KU-472-272

Rough Justice

When four officers of the law are slaughtered in a bloody battle with two hillbilly rustlers, US Marshal Heck Thomas and his new deputy, Zeke, head for Indian Territory on their trail.

At Fort Smith, Judge Parker is executing criminals, six at a time, and Heck decides that it is time to impose some rough justice of his own.

Why, he wonders, does the notorious Belle Starr, with her clan of gun-crazy Cherokees, always escape the noose? Why does the Hanging Judge ride out to a lonesome cabin in the woods and what secret does he hide? Can the marshal lure Belle and her boys into a trap?

Carbines blaze and the body count spirals as Heck and Zeke put their lives on the line to find out.

By the same author

Hogan's Bunch
Double Action
Trouble at Taos
Anderson's War

Rough Justice

Jackson Davis

AS — Dumfries and Galloway LIBRARIES

1 5 7 8 7 1 | Class WE

A Black Horse Western

ROBERT HALE · LONDON

© Jackson Davis 2010
First published in Great Britain 2010

ISBN 978-0-7090-8881-3

Robert Hale Limited
Clerkenwell House
Clerkenwell Green
London EC1R 0HT

www.halebooks.com

The right of Jackson Davis to be identified as
author of this work has been asserted by him
in accordance with the Copyright, Designs and
Patents Act 1988

Typeset by
Derek Doyle & Associates, Shaw Heath
Printed and bound in Great Britain by
CPI Antony Rowe, Chippenham and Eastbourne

ONE

Fort Smith was in festive mood as young Zeke Jones rode his Appaloosa into the town on the bank of the wide Arkansas River. He weaved his way through a crowd that had come from far and wide, jumped down, hitched the horse to a rail, and brushed down his tight-legged, three-piece Sunday suit. 'Waal, I'll be danged!' He gave a whistle of awe. 'Just look at these!'

The objects of his admiration were three young ladies decked in the height of fashion, with large fancy hats, concoctions of feathers and lace, perched saucily on their heads. Arm in arm, they were swinging along the sidewalk towards him.

Zeke tipped back his Stetson to hang from its cord on his back, pushed fingers through his thatch of blond hair, and sprang up onto the sidewalk to accost them. 'Howdy, gals. Where ya going?'

'Where ya think we're going?' one retorted. 'Where everybody else is going. To the hangings.'

'Step outa the way, junior,' the older, more sharp-faced of the three ordered. 'We ain't got no time to waste with riff-raff.'

'I ain't riff-raff. I'm gonna be a marshal,' Zeke drawled, for he had come to Fort Smith to enrol with its elite force of lawmen.

'Mercy!' The prettiest of the trio smirked at him. 'What you gonna do? Arrest us in our beds?'

All three were attired in ankle-length skirts and little bolero jackets buttoned tight against the cold breeze off the river. 'Come on,' the older one urged, 'or we'll miss the party.'

But the pretty one held back, cocked her head to one side, appraising him. 'You know how to use that thang?' She nodded at the Smith & Wesson revolver hung over his loins. 'Or is it just for show?'

She had a mass of reddish ringlets about a somewhat chubby, snub-nosed face beneath the preposterous hat. For some reason her remark made them all burst into laughter and suddenly Zeke became tongue-tied with confusion.

'How many desperadoes you gunned down with that?'

'Waal, 'he stuttered, 'none so far. I ain't started yet.'

'Aw, ain't that sweet,' the sharp-faced woman cooed. 'He's a virgin. Shall we help him out, gals?'

'Depends what he's got in his pocket?' the third girl mused. 'You know what these country boys are like. Most just got a hole in it.'

'Don't take no notice.' As the other two giggled, the pretty girl broke away from them, slipped her arm in his and said, 'We're hurdies along at the Horse's Leg saloon. My name's Pearl. Come on, I'll show you the scene.'

The six men standing in line on the gallows were a motley bunch, one black, two young white tearaways, a couple of half-breeds, and a full-blood Indian, aptly named Smoking Mankiller, for he had shot down one of the posse of US deputy marshals who caught up with the gang on the banks of the Red River. All were found guilty of homicide, cattle rustling and robbery with violence.

The bald-headed, bushy-bearded hangman,

George Maledon, was tightening the nooses about their necks. He disappeared below the high gallows, pulled a lever, and the packed crowd of onlookers seemed to give a communal sigh as the six condemned dropped simultaneously.

'Serve 'em right,' a woman shrieked. 'They were killers, all of 'em.'

The gallows stood in front of a large, imposing building which served as courthouse, offices and judge's accommodation, with prison cells in the basement. As the crowd began drifting away to carouse in Fort Smith's saloons, Judge Isaac Parker stood at his study window with a sombre expression before turning away, too.

'Is that Marshal Thomas over there?' Zeke pointed to a tall man with a bushy walrus moustache, who was by the gallows. 'I gotta go volunteer.'

Pearl hugged his arm. 'Hi, Marshal, here's a new recruit.'

Heck Thomas frowned at her. 'You behaving yourself, Pearl?'

'Oh, yes.' She gave him a sweet smile, her eyes full of mockery. 'I'm a good li'l girl.'

They watched her go wiggling away to join her two pals. 'She a friend of yours?' Heck asked.

'Yes, suh. What a beaut, eh? Only met her today but she sure set my heart palpitating.'

'I bet that ain't the only organ she set palpitating,' the hangman growled, as he oiled the long platform of the gallows which allowed half-a-dozen candidates to enter the next world in unison.

'You want to join the service?' the marshal asked.

'Yes, suh. I was born in the saddle. Got my own hoss and revolver.' He whipped the Smith & Wesson from its holster and plugged the dangling Mankiller between the eyes. 'How's that?'

'Hey, you show some respect to my corpses,' Maledon cried, as the explosion reverberated away.

Thomas smiled. 'Quick draw, kid, huh? We'll see. First maybe you can help Mr Maledon bury his corpses in the lime pit. Then we'll see how you are with a carbine.'

'Jeez.' Zeke stared at the dangling six. 'Makes ya think, don't it? They dropped straight through the trap into the flaming pit of hell.'

'Grab hold of this un and raise him up,' the hangman shouted, releasing a noose as Zeke did so. 'Now chuck him in my pit.'

*

Judge Parker was an imposing man, six feet tall and weighing 200lbs, with neatly combed, luxuriant black hair, clean-shaven but for a jutting goatee beard.

After he had sworn Zeke in he gave him his badge and book of rules. 'Study and abide by these,' he warned solemnly. 'What's your opinion, Mr Thomas?'

'He put five outa six shots centre target with the carbine at two hundred yards.' Heck smiled. 'He's a tad wild, but I believe he'll make a good deputy marshal.'

'Good.' The judge glowered at Zeke. 'You follow Mr Thomas's example and you won't go far wrong.'

'Time for a snifter?' George Maledon was tamping down the pit. He chucked his shovel aside, buckled a brace of pistols in a belt about the waist of his suit, and led the way out of the stockade. They went along the river's waterfront, dodging through wagons and horses, and workers busy unloading bales of cotton to be rolled into the holds of awaiting steamboats which plied their trade on the Arkansas.

The trio found a table in a back room of an

emporium run by China Sue amid a clutter of sacks of dry goods and spices, oriental pottery and nick-nacks. She put a bottle of rice wine with three tumblers before them.

George smacked his lips, as he paid Sue a silver dollar. 'I'll cover this.'

'Guess you can afford to,' Heck remarked. 'At a hundred dollars a hanging you must be the wealthiest guy in Fort Smith. It ain't a job I could do. Don't it give you the willies, George?'

'Willies? Why should it? I take pride in a job well done. All you, me and the judge are doing is cleaning up the mess that Indian Territory has become. Willies? Pah! What, for dropping them six vile villains? No, sir.'

'I guess Deputy Spivey has been avenged.'

'True.' George raised his glass. 'A good officer cut down in the prime of life. What does give me the willies is when them dirty, li'l, dog-dick lawyers start spouting their legal mumbo jumbo. Remember, boy, you ain't s'posed to shoot some mad dog murderer on sight. No, you gotta read them their rights, or they'll appeal and get death commuted to life.'

Heck laughed. 'And do you outa your hanging fee.' The marshal noticed his recruit seemed miles away. 'You'll have to excuse Zeke. He got hit by Cupid's dart today. Guess who, George?'

'Pearl Starr? You need to steer clear of that l'il hussy, boy. She's trouble.'

'Why?' Zeke looked startled. 'What are you talking about?'

'You know who she is, doncha?' Maledon demanded. 'Belle Starr's only daughter. Yes, Belle, the bitch who presides over that nest of rattlers out at Younger's Bend.'

'What?' Zeke stuttered his surprise. 'But that don't mean Pearl . . . she's such a sweet girl.'

'Boy,' George scoffed. 'You're living in Cloud Cuckoo Land.'

TWO

Across the border from Fort Smith was the vast Indian Territory, 34,000 square miles set aside as a homeland for numerous tribes. The five civilized tribes, the Cherokee, Choctaw, Creek, Chickasaw and Seminole had settled the eastern part, a place of great scenic beauty, wooded hills and valleys threaded by rivers, lakes and waterfalls. The Cherokee had taken to white people's ways, even their clothes, marketing corn and cotton, breeding horses and cattle, with their own newspaper and tribal courts.

But with the Civil War had come chaos, some Cherokee slave holders supporting the Confederates, others fighting for the Union. Since then many Cherokee had gone to the bad, as had numerous freed slaves, as the Territory became the hideout for disaffected Confederates and fugitive white killers.

Belle Starr might have had a college education, been taught the piano, French and Greek, but she was one of the worst. When a pair of illiterate, scruffy hillbillies, Jim and Pink Lee, turned up at her husband's sixty-acre spread with a herd of rustled Cherokee horses she had paid them fifty dollars, quickly had her men alter the brands and headed north for the border. In Kansas she pocketed a sweet $450 profit. Life was pretty good. . . .

As Zeke Jones chomped his supper in the barracks behind the courthouse, his thoughts were fixated on Pearl Starr. Unable to rest, he hurried out to look for her at the Horse's Leg, one of the thirty saloons and dance places that catered for Fort Smith's 30,000 population. He was glad that, at least, she did not work The Row, a line of shacks where whores plied their trade. The judge had decreed that these women should not be allowed to roam the streets after 9 p.m., or solicit in the saloons at any time without risk of a hefty fine.

A former congressman, the judge was a strict Methodist. His wife, Mary, was a bit of a bluenose, a do-gooder, who hoped to open a home for these fallen ladies. Kind treatment and prayer would, she was sure, save them from their sinful ways.

Pearl, the 18-year-old Zeke was sure, could not be one of those. But, sure enough, the Horse's Leg was where she was.

His heart missed a beat as he pushed into the crowded dance house and saw Pearl behind a pole fence among other hurdy-gurdy gals. She was chatting animatedly to two rough-looking *hombres* who were leaning over the pole.

Zeke screwed up his courage, strolled across the dance floor and called, 'Hi!'

'Well' – she gave her mocking, sparkling smile – 'if it ain't the virgin deputy.'

Zeke felt the blood rushing to his face again as the two men turned to stare at him, scornfully. 'Can I have a dance?' he blurted out.

'What, with them?' she asked, mischievously, indicating the hardcases.

'No, you.' He showed her a ticket he had bought from the kiosk by the door. 'Or are you busy?'

'No, I'm anybody's,' she said, standing up. 'Five cents a dance. Sure you can afford me?'

Pearl had divested herself of her jacket and was wearing a blue silk blouse tucked into her long skirt. The band of trumpet, guitar and drums was blaring out some kind of Mexican melody, so Zeke grabbed her and went gallomphing around in his heavy boots, bumping shoulders with others in the giddy whirl.

'You certainly haven't been to any dancing academy, have you?' she remarked as she skipped about to avoid having her toes trod on. 'What's this, the Texas two-step?'

'It's the only dance I know.' He held her tighter, amazed to feel the warmth of her firm bosom pressing against his chest as Pearl hung on and the boards bounced.

'I got another ticket,' he said, as the number ended. In fact, he had four more tickets and grabbed her tighter every time she agreed to another spin. 'I just wanted to tell you, Pearl,' he said, 'I really like you.'

'You're not so bad, yourself. Otherwise I wouldn't be letting you monopolize me.'

'I mean, I really, really like you.' It was a slower melody and they were pressed real tight, the touch of the girl's body having its effect on him.

'Yeah, I can tell that.' Pearl gave her cheeky grin.

16

'Or is that your gun sticking in me?'

He finally disentangled himself from her and followed her back to her bench. 'Couldn't we go somewhere quiet to talk?' He had to shout to be heard as he leaned over the pole what with the racket of the band and a bunch of drunken rowdies at the bar. 'I've got to get back to the barracks before ten, 'fore they lock up.'

'Too bad.' She slipped away to dance with an old galoot as Zeke watched. 'You still here?' She grimaced, when she got back. 'My poor feet!'

'Do you live here?'

'I got a room upstairs. But I ain't allowed to take boys up there.'

'Can I see you tomorrow night?'

'Why not?' She smiled and gave a little wave as she was whisked away again. 'I'm off early at eight. Maybe we can arrange something.'

At 5 a.m. the bugle sounded 'Boots and Saddles'. Zeke was one of seven officers chosen by Marshal Thomas to ride out with him into the Nations. A report had come in of horses stolen from the Cherokee. As he mounted up to head 130 miles up-river to Fort Gibson and on to the Cherokee capital, Tahlaqua, Zeke wondered for the hundredth time just what Pearl Starr had had in mind. Now, perhaps, he would never know.

THREE

'All right, boys.' Marshal Heck Thomas raised a hand to slow the posse as they rode along beside the snow-swollen Canadian River. 'It ain't far to Younger's Bend now. Check your weapons. Have 'em at the ready. You never know what reception we might get.'

A paunchy veteran, Marshal Jim Guy, levered his Winchester carbine and clacked a .44 from the magazine into the breech. 'Yeah,' he growled. 'I say we clean out this cesspit of scum. They've terrorized the whole area for too long.'

'Steady, Jim,' Heck warned. 'You know the judge's rules. If they give us any trouble we got to take them back alive for him to hang.'

'Some hope of that,' Frank Dalton scoffed.

'We've taken that hard-faced bitch and her crew in before. Huccome she allus manages to wriggle off the hook?'

He was referring to Belle Starr, her sobriquet, Queen of the Bandits, well-earned. Since marrying the full-blood Cherokee, Sam Starr, she had been responsible for numerous killings, robberies and countless acts of cattle rustling.

'Yeah, how come we've never made a prosecution stick?' Deputy Marshal Abe Burrows put in. 'I agree with Big Jim. We should put 'em to the flames and have done with it.'

'That's enough of that talk,' Marshal Thomas snapped. 'For the benefit of you new boys we all know Belle's a mistress at bribing and intimidating witnesses and jurors and even court officials. That's why she ain't never served any time. They don't call her The Fixer for nothing. But there'll be no shooting unless I say so. We're here looking for evidence.'

Zeke tipped back his Stetson and scratched at his thick mop of blond hair. 'I ain't clear about this, Mr Thomas. If any of 'em take a pot at us, do we wait for your command before we retaliate?'

'No, of course we don't,' Big Jim roared. 'If they start shooting we shoot back. And we don't stop 'til

20

they're all dead.'

'That's enough, Jim. I'm giving the orders here.' Marshal Thomas, in his dark suit, and high-bowled hat, clean-shaven but for his luxuriant moustache, looked more like a businessman than a legendary shootist and thief-taker. 'These Cherokee can be pretty volatile, but I think Belle's too cute to let 'em give us trouble.'

The posse were all attired in dark suits, a uniform the Hanging Judge imposed on his men, most of them with wide-brimmed hats, bandannas, and duster coats or wind-shedders for, although it was late April, winter departed slowly in these parts.

They walked their horses warily as the ramshackle barns, outhouses, corrals and ranch-house at Younger's Bend came into view. It was tucked away into a knoll of the hills and smoke was spiralling from one of the chimneys.

Heck Thomas halted his men, raised a pocket telescope to his eye and examined the place. A scruffy half-breed, a feather in his high-topped hat, was prowling about on his pony at the entrance gate, a rifle in one hand.

'He's seen us,' Heck said, returning the glass to his pocket. 'Come on. We're going in. Once we're in the yard, fan out and be ready to dive for cover. Zeke, you keep your eyes on the house windows; Josh, you cover the hayloft. Watch out for back-shooters.'

The other new recruit, a fresh-faced Jewish boy, Josh Abrahams, glanced at Zeke apprehensively, as he clutched his government issue carbine and urged his scrubby mount forward. 'Sure thang, Mr Thomas.'

Zeke's heart had begun pounding hard at the possibility of his first taste of action as he followed on his Appaloosa. 'We got ya.'

The posse's caution proved an anti-climax. Belle Starr was sitting side-saddle on her grey mare, Venus, all innocence and smiles. 'Morning, Mr Thomas,' she called. 'What brings you to these parts? I was just about to go for my morning ride.'

Belle affected a wide-skirted English riding habit, a tight-buttoned topcoat and stock, and sported a velour hat, pinned up on one side, with a trailing ostrich feather, cavalier-style. She rode about the Territory far and wide with impunity, visiting low dives and out-of-the way corners where others might fear to tread, often in the past with her young daughter, Pearl, in tow. Belle liked to spend her ill-gotten gains generously among a favoured few.

'You know what's brought us here well enough,' Heck replied. 'We're looking for them forty stolen horses. They were communal property of the Cherokee at Tahlaqua. What you done with 'em, Belle?'

'Stolen horses.' There was mockery in Belle's eyes, dark and bright as blueberries. 'What you talking about, Marshal?'

'You bastards can clear out.' Old Tom Starr, her father-in-law, had skulked out onto the wooden veranda of the two-storey house. His greying hair was tied back in a pony-tail, and he wore the torn grey frock coat of the former Cherokee Mounted Rifles. Slave-holder and supporter of the South, he had led a murderous, breakaway guerilla brigade in the Civil War and would often boast of a family he had burned alive in their house. 'This is my land. You're abusing my tribal rights. You got no jurisdiction here.'

'Throw that shotgun down,' Heck shouted, 'or we'll blast you to hell.'

The house door creaked open and his son, a tall Cherokee, Sam Starr, stepped out. In a black suit and white collarless shirt, his black hair reaching to his shoulders, he soothed, 'OK, Pa, we have no fight with the marshal.'

'These scum have no right here,' Tom snarled, but reluctantly surrendered the twelve gauge. Sam tossed it forward into the mud.

'You Starrs are the scum,' Deputy Marshal Bill Neames cried out. 'You prey on your own people.'

The man on guard was still sitting his pony, rifle in hand, and had skulked away to take a position alongside old Tom. Others of their men had moved forward from the corrals and bunkhouse, and one emerged leading a nag from the barn.

The deputies had them covered with their carbines and Frank Dalton shouted, 'All of you. Throw down your weapons. Line up in front of the house. You, too, Tom. Revolvers, knives, everything. Snap to it unless you want a taste of lead.'

'This is outrageous,' Belle cried. 'Judge Parker will hear about this.'

'We're acting on his orders,' Heck Thomas replied, sternly. 'The two Lee brothers stole forty horses and they were followed and seen driving them into this ranch.'

'Oh, *those* horses. Why didn't you say so, marshal?' Belle cooed sweetly. 'Those wicked men did bring them here. I can't think why. What would I want with all those horses? I told them to clear

24

off, pronto.' She waved her whip in a northerly direction. 'They went thataway.'

Big Jim Guy swung down from his horse and herded the men together in front of the house, brandishing his carbine. 'Get in line,' he said. He jabbed the carbine butt hard into the belly of the guard who had stepped from his pony, making him gasp, double up and curse. Jim knocked the rifle from his hand and brought his carbine barrel round to connect with his jaw, showering teeth. 'Get down on your face. Quick!'

'You will die for this,' the half-breed muttered, spitting blood, but lay spread-eagled as Jim kicked him and removed a knife from his boot. 'Thought as much,' Jim muttered, tossing it away. 'Anybody else want the same treatment?'

Sam Starr threw down his revolver and scalping knife. 'There's no need for this, Marshal. We're offering no resistance.'

'You better not,' Josh Abrahams growled, 'or you won't be seein' tomorrow.'

'What's going on, Ma?' a plaintive voice wailed. Belle's son poked his head out of a first-floor window. He disappeared quickly as Zeke swung around and sent a slug whistling to smash the woodwork.

25

'Go get him, Zeke,' Jim Guy roared.

'No need for that,' Heck shouted. 'He's harmless.'

'None of these skunks is harmless,' Guy said.

But a pasty-faced youth, looking like he'd crawled out of a hedge backwards, wearing only a filthy pair of long johns, waved a pair of his mother's white cotton drawers out of the front door, screaming, 'Don't shoot, please! Gawd no! I'm comin' out.'

'Another of Belle's spawn,' Deputy Abe Burrows commented. 'Wonder who *his* daddy was? Damned sure it couldn't have been Cole Younger. He couldn't have fathered such a yellow cur.'

'He always was a slug-a-bed, that boy,' Belle smirked, as she looked over at her son who had joined the line shivering and shaking. 'Don't worry, darling. These gentlemen will soon be gone. They've made a mistake.'

'Don't be so sure of that,' Thomas replied. 'Search the place, boys. You step down, too, Mrs Starr. Take that hardware out from under your coat.'

'What? This?' Belle jumped lightly from the mare and produced a .45 Colt, handing it over by the barrel. 'I clean forgot.' She removed her wide-brimmed, feathered hat with a flourish. 'Perhaps you'd better look in this, too, for concealed weapons. You're wasting your time, Mr Thomas.'

Zeke turned to take a look at her. He guessed she was in her late thirties, which to him was real old. But at the same time there was something slim and sensuous about her. Her dark hair was tied back into a bun, and there were scars of – what? – depravity, on her once pretty face. But he could see why so many men found her sexy. Maybe it was her reputation, her attitude, the challenge in her eyes.

'You don't think I'm stupid enough to keep any stolen property on the premises, even if I had any,' she said, scornfully. 'I heard on the grapevine days ago that you were coming. Maybe you'd better rake through the river.'

Thomas emptied her revolver and returned it to her.

'Thank you,' she said, turning to meet Zeke's regard. 'What's this? You lost so many men you're enrolling boys these days? Hi, handsome. You ever need a job you come an' see me. You'll get paid better and have more fun' – she gave him a wink as she went to stand beside her husband – 'know what I mean?'

Zeke strolled over to her. 'It's your daughter, Pearl, I'm crazy about. What if I said I'd like to wed her?'

'Yee-hoo!' Belle stamped her foot and punched the air. 'You hear that, boys? The deputy wants to marry Pearl. We'll have a lawman in the family.'

'Over my dead body,' Old Tom snarled.

'Yes, we oughta celebrate. But we cain't.' Belle hoped Tom had his jugs of whiskey well hidden. 'We ain't allowed licker in the Nations.'

'We ain't even allowed to scalp our enemies any more,' Tom said. 'Who do these whiteys think they are?' He pointed at Big Jim. 'As for you, you will be dead soon. I can read it on your face. And you others. You ain't got long.'

'That's enough,' Marshal Thomas shouted. 'Let's start searching this place.'

He stepped down, caught hold of Zeke's arm and whispered, 'What are you playing at?'

Zeke winked at him. 'Thought it would be a good idea to get in with 'em, suh.'

'Forget it, Zeke. Let's take a look. I can smell whiskey here.'

But, as projected by Belle, the search proved fruitless.

'What's the damn use?' Thomas snapped.

'Mount up, men. We're moving out of here.'

The Starrs gave an ironic cheer as they watched the Federals ride out. 'Bastards!' Old Tom summed up.

'They'll find no trace of those horses.' Belle climbed onto Venus. She looked around, imperiously, at the men. She was the brains behind this outfit and they knew it. She tossed a pouch of gold coins at Sam. 'Here! You better pay the boys.'

FOUR

The posse rode circling 500 miles north, calling in at Muskogee, riding along the shores of the Cherokee Lake, following the old Shawnee trail, crossing the Cimarron River, reaching the Kansas border at Baxter Springs, circling west through the Wichita mountains, then back south, making enquiries in Pawnee and Ponca cities, but there were no signs, no reports of the stolen Cherokee horses.

The lawmen were greeted sullenly, for if a man did know anything would he want to be dragged into Fort Smith to give evidence in court without any witness's expenses? The Starrs were either too clever at covering their tracks, or too feared, or maybe the marshals had been looking in the wrong places, but the fact was they had drawn a blank. True they had found a couple of running irons, used to cleverly alter brands, at the Starrs' ranch, but that would be hardly enough to gain a conviction.

So, after spending a night at the quiet little hamlet of Tulsey Town – later to be known as Tulsa – they pointed their horses' noses back towards Muskogee and Fort Gibson, following the meandering Cimarron.

They rested the night at the military post. After supper, Big Jim remarked caustically, 'Just think of our six cents a mile for trailing outlaws. Ain't we doing well? Plus our two dollars arrest fee, just supposing we arrest anybody.'

'You gotta look on the bright side,' Zeke said. 'At least it ain't snowing.'

'Pah! We put our lives on the line for a pittance. Still, I don't suppose that worries you, young feller. You just joined the force for the glory.'

Big Jim had served his time honourably, but like others was soured by the opinion they were not paid their true worth. On average, a marshal would be lucky to rake in as much as $500 a year. If they killed a violent prisoner attempting escape they would be forced to pay the man's funeral expenses.

'Maybe there'll be some reward money on these

31

Lee brothers,' Zeke suggested. 'Won't we all get a share if we catch 'em?'

The half-dozen federal men guffawed at his greeness. 'There's five hundred on Jim for stage robbery and a thousand on Pink for murder and rape committed in Texas. But they're government rewards,' Heck explained. 'As gov'ment employees we ain't entitled to 'em.'

'That don't seem fair,' young Zeke mused.

When they all chuckled again at his naïvety, Heck soothed, 'Don't let it dampen your ardour, Zeke.'

'Sounds like these Lee brothers could be dangerous,' young Josh Abrahams remarked. 'Know anythang about 'em, Heck?'

'Aw, they're just a coupla hillbillies,' Thomas replied. 'They shouldn't give us much trouble. We gotta find 'em first.'

'Lo and behold!' the marshal cried, as they rode south the next morning. He peered through his telescope at two riders approaching along the river-bank.'I'll be danged, if it ain't the Lees.'

'You sure?' Frank Dalton asked.

'Sure I'm sure. I'd recognize those two li'l runts anywhere.'

The two horsemen, apparently, were having doubts about the approaching eight-man posse for they, too, had pulled in their broncos. Suddenly they spun their mounts and went haring back the way they had come.

'Come on, boys,' Heck yelled, spurring his quarter horse away. 'The race is on.'

'Yay-hoo!' Zeke screamed, quick off the mark on his Appaloosa, going streaking after their leader as the others pounded along behind. 'We got 'em.'

Heck's quarter horse had a fantastic turn of speed over a quarter of a mile, and he was way out in front. The Appaloosa, favourite hunting mount of the Nez Perce Indians could almost match him.

As if realizing that they could never outrun them, the Lees were turning their mustangs away from the river and climbing up a rocky incline towards the treeline.

'Where did they come from?' Pink Lee shouted, as he reached the cover of a stand of dark pines and some handy rocks to hide behind, pulling his mustang round the back to tether him. He drew from his bedroll his large-frame Colt Lightning rifle, his tobacco-rasping lungs wheezing from the chase. He looked down the slope at the posse which was still half a mile away, but which had reached the incline and was spreading out as the deputies chose their own routes to urge their horses up after them. 'Damn fools. I know where they can go – on into hell.'

Pink settled down, resting the Lightning's long barrel on a v-notch of two rocks, adjusting the sights, feeding a big .50-.95 express calibre cartridge into the breech, bringing a grimy handful of others from his topcoat pocket to line up on a rock for use.

Beside him his brother, Jim, had a similar maniacal look in his eyes as he prepared his new Marlin rifle which he figured was the equal of any Winchester. 'What 'n hail can they do to us with them puny carbines?'

Both brothers knew they had to hit the lawmen hard and fast before they got in close. Pink gave a toothless grin as he lovingly took first pressure on his trigger, then squeezed and, with the clap of an explosion, sent one of his big slugs whistling towards the deputies. It had the power to kill a buffalo at that range. New recruit Josh Abrahams would not have known a lot about it as the bullet crashed through his chest and severed his spine.

'Got him!' Pink howled, as Abrahams threw up

his arms and collapsed into the scrub. 'This is gonna be like potting ducks.'

Jim had not been so lucky but his .45-.70 cut through the neck of Dalton's mustang and it screamed as blood gouted, going over, legs flailing, trapping Frank beneath its body.

'That'll teach 'em to come after us Lees,' Jim cried.

He had hardly spoken before his brother, Pink, rocketed out another slug that took away half of Abe Burrows' head in a mess of flying bone, brain and blood.

'Yee-hagh!' Pink let out a shrill rebel yell. He was elated. It was like being back in the war taking out the hated federal men.

Heck Thomas was more fortunate. Jim Lee's next shot merely sent his high hat spinning. He looked around, desperately, as his men were decimated. 'Take cover,' he yelled, jumping from his quarter horse.

Heck crouched in the rocks reassessing the situation. He had made a bad mistake underestimating the Lees. 'Thought they were just a couple of crazy hillbillies,' he muttered to Zeke, who was nearby. 'Seems like these boys are crack shots.'

'What we gonna do?' Zeke gritted out, as another large calibre bullet sent a small pine crashing almost on top of him.

'We've got to get up closer.' Heck fired his revolver up at the men in the trees but he knew he was wasting his ammunition. 'We've got to get within range,' he shouted to any of his men still alive who could hear him. 'Try to get up behind them.'

Bill Neames was eager to prove his worth. He jumped up and, at a crouch went haring up the slope as the deputies covered him with a hail of lead from their carbines.

But it was no good. The Lees had chosen their spot well. They were protected by the rocks and the shadow of the dark, low-hanging pines. Pink calmly took aim as the young deputy came zig-zagging up the slope. The onslaught of lead hissing and cutting about Pink's head did not faze him. His sights hovered on Neames and he pulled the trigger of the Colt Lightning.

'Bull's eye.' he cried, as Bill went bouncing back down the slope to lay prostrate, his heart blasted apart.

Pink gave a hysterical laugh. 'Howja like that, Marshal? Anyone else wanna try?'

Zeke pumped the last of his twelve .44s at the clouds of black smoke rolling out from the trees and laid low to reload the Winchester magazine. 'I ain't keen on these odds,' he muttered. 'But we can't give up now. We got to get up there.'

There was some sporadic fire as the remaining federal men kept their heads down, chastened by the punishment, and tried to crawl up closer to the treeline. They managed to reach an overhanging rock where they gathered together.

Marshal Thomas had been under far worse fire than this as a drummer boy in the war, beating out the tattoo, stepping on and over sprawled bodies as balls fizzed past his head and soldiers dropped all about him. Maybe that experience gave him his steely will, his determination to go stubbornly on until the battle was won or lost.

'OK, boys,' he croaked out. 'Y'all ready for another push? When I say go we all charge. We gotta finish this.'

But it was the Lees who finished it. The line of possemen came pounding up the slope but the two brothers faced their fire even though they were now only a hundred yards away. First in the line was the burly veteran, Marshal Jim Guy. He roared his desperation as he ran straight into one of Pink's bullets and was catapulted back down the slope. Jim Lee's slug hit a deputy called Wally Love in the thigh and he gasped as he tumbled to his knees.

'Down!' Heck shouted, hitting the dust as once again they were stopped in their tracks. He listened and waited, his heart pounding, getting his breath back. It had gone uncannily quiet. 'Come on,' he shouted. 'One last push.'

Crouching low, Zeke raced up towards the trees, but just before he reached them he glanced along and saw the Lees on their mustangs, their rifles in their hands, riding hell for leather away along the ridge. Within seconds they were over the top and gone.

All that was left to greet Heck Thomas was a pile of empty shell casings. He picked them up and examined the calibres. 'Damn,' he hissed. 'This is bad.'

It was time to do what they could for Wally Love, bind his leg and help him back down the slope. Heck Thomas stood over the body of Big Jim Guy. 'He was a good man. He's got a wife and four kids at home.'

'Aren't we going after 'em?' Zeke asked.

'Ain't four men dead enough for one day?'

Heck replied. 'We've got to get these boys' bodies back to Fort Smith so they can have honourable burials.'

They climbed disconsolately back down the slope to peer at the bloody remains of Abe, Josh and Bill.

Heck stared up at the ridge the way the Lees had gone. The two outlaws knew all the backtrails. They would be well away.

'We'll be avenged,' Heck promised. 'Them two ain't gonna get away with this.'

Suddenly he heard a cry from down in the scrub. 'Aw, I'd forgotten all about Frank. We gotta get him out from under his hoss.'

FIVE

Back at Fort Smith, Judge Isaac Parker was having his own problems. *The Washington Journal* and other Eastern newspapers were lambasting his six-at-a-time public hangings as 'a degrading spectacle unworthy of these modern times'.

The pile of week-old news-sheets had arrived from the capital marked for his attention and, after dinner with his wife and two boys, he was reading through them. 'What utter poppycock!' he snorted. 'These people have no idea what life is like out here.'

He had been appointed to his position by President Ulysses Grant who had urged him to 'get things straightened out'. That was what Parker intended to do even if it meant straightening a good number of worthless necks.

Six days a week, from 8 a.m. to 6 p.m. he had sat in his court house dispensing justice to what appeared to be a never-ending array of the dregs of humanity. Only that day he had dealt with an evader of town taxes, a prostitute drunk and disorderly in one of the saloons, and a 98-year-old man, John Overton, guilty of defrauding his neighbour. 'Go home,' Parker told him, 'and sin no more.' Well, he could hardly put him in prison.

Parker believed in tempering justice with mercy, but not for killers like Patrick Doonan who had come up before him the day before. He had raped and killed a farmer's wife and deserved the noose.

'They say I lead juries,' Parker protested. 'Well, of course, I lead juries. They are there to be led. I certainly never fail to let them know when I deem a man is guilty. All these legal niceties, these appeals, this Blackstone finicketyness, it makes me sick.'

'But Isaac,' Mary replied, 'you must admit your decisions are very severe. Whatever a man has done he can surely be brought to repentance? What right have we to take his life? Look at that nice Mr Doonan down there in those squalid cells this very moment awaiting the walk to your gallows. He tells me he committed that awful murder while possessed by the demon rum. He wants to wash away his sins in the blood of Jesus Christ.'

'Mary!' Parker thundered. 'I have expressly forbidden you. How many times must I tell you to leave my prisoners alone? So, you've been down there again?'

'Husband, you cannot forbid me from spreading the message of the Lord. Yes, I have been reading the gospels to Mr Doonan through his cell bars and praying with him.'

A compassionate woman, Mary felt deeply for the wretches crushed into the two common cells in the basement, a prison putrid with the smell of urinal tubs, disease, sweat and tobacco. She had often dared, while the judge was occupied in court, to go down the stone steps to take small creature comforts to them.

'Do you know what that *nice* man did, Mary?' The judge scowled at her. 'He beat and tortured her husband, then forced him to watch as he dragged that poor woman away from her babies, and raped her before their eyes, then he slit her throat.'

'Isaac, please, your language. Think of the boys.'

Their two young sons were sitting opposite, wide-eyed, listening. 'I'm sure Mr Doonan was possessed of the Devil. Have you no sympathy?'

'Sympathy?' Parker roared. 'I save my sympathy for the families made fatherless and motherless by these drunken, violent assassins. I think of the honest, noble men like my officers cut down pursuing their duties. Already we have lost forty-six deputy marshals in my stay here. I think of the farmers and ranchers, the backbone of this country, their horses and cattle rustled, their savings stolen; they and their kin shot down by these greedy evil men who come before me. All this sympathy you talk about is sad, sentimental, misdirected poppycock.'

He hurled the papers aside and strode to the door of his study. 'I have work to do. It's time the boys were in bed.'

But, about ten, unable to concentrate, he put the books and papers aside, and took his candle out into the silent, darkened apartment. He checked the boys were asleep, then hesitated, his hand closing over the knob of his wife's bedroom door. Since a difficult second birth Mary had insisted on sleeping alone.

He quietly opened the door and stepped inside,

placing the flickering candle on the bedside table and sitting down gently on the bed. Mary was asleep, or pretending to be, breathing gently, her face benign in the floppy nightcap, her flannel nightdress buttoned modestly to the throat. Suddenly her eyes opened with a startled look.

'Isaac! What do you want?'

Wasn't it obvious, the judge thought. He was a virile man in the prime of life. 'Mary,' he murmured, stroking her cheek. 'I am sorry I spoke harshly to you. I thought, perhaps, we. . . ?'

'Isaac.' The knuckles of her hands tightened on the quilt as if she would hang onto it against all odds and her face and whole body taughtened. She had always been an awkward woman to make love to at the best of times. 'No, you promised me,' she simpered, in a little-girl voice. 'You said we would only do that at Thanksgiving and Yuletide.'

'But, surely . . .' The judge sighed and turned away. He knew there was no use appealing the sentence. He stared into the darkness for moments, picked up the candle and went to his own room.

Judge Parker was about to go into court the next morning when he heard shouting, some sort of ruckus down in the cells and a woman's scream. His heart froze. It could only be Mary.

'Hand over the fockin' keys,' Doonan shouted to the gaoler. 'If not, she's a dead woman.'

Parker clattered down the stone steps and saw his wife's agonized face as Doonan held her with one arm through the bars around her bosom, the other pricking an iron spike hard against her throat. 'How dare you?' he shouted. 'Let her go.'

'Sure, I'll let the ugly bitch go.' Doonan grinned at him. 'Just as soon as you get this gate opened and a horse and gun ready and waiting for me at the door.'

'Never,' Parker growled, but he knew he had no choice.

Doonan hurled a string of obscenities at him. 'You ain't hangin' me, Parker, you bloodthirsty butcher. I'm out of here. Then nobody gets hurt, not even her, the silly cow, coming down here with her jellies and flowers and Bible praying. Don't she make you sick? Maybe you'd rather I killed her? It don't worry me.'

'Please, Isaac,' Mary croaked out. 'Help me.'

Parker met her eyes for moments. 'All right, gaoler. Do as he says.'

Suddenly a shot crashed out. A crimson hole

appeared in Doonan's forehead and started gushing blood. Then he tottered back and collapsed.

Judge Parker turned around and saw the hangman, George Maledon, standing at the top of the stairs, his eyes burning like some avenging god of old. A smoking revolver was in his outstretched right hand, another at the ready in his left.

'Good Lord,' Parker remonstrated. 'You could have killed Mary.'

'I didn't though, did I?' Maledon muttered through his beard. 'I just did myself out of a hundred-dollar hanging fee.'

Parker calmed his hysterical wife and half-carried her up the stairs. He turned and announced, 'This is between us. No word to anyone else. We mustn't let the newspapers hear about this. It is all they need, George. Or you'll be losing a lot more hanging fees.'

SIX

'The judge ain't gonna like this,' Heck Thomas gritted out, as he and Zeke Jones rode their horses back into Fort Smith, followed by a two-horse flatbed wagon driven by the injured Deputy Wally Love. Lying inside was Frank Dalton, with his broken leg, and the corpses of their four colleagues.

Rattling along behind was a horse and wagon driven by Gaylord Cooper, a stubble-chinned, rosy-nosed rum peddler. His wrists and ankles were manacled with chains. In the canvas-covered cart behind him were assorted bottles and barrels of liquor he had been planning to sell to the tribes and Anglo badmen of Indian Territory before he had the misfortune to bump into Heck and his remaining marshals.

He was the only fish they had caught, much to Heck's chagrin. Not so long before he had returned in triumph leading a caravan of wagons and unloaded thirty-two prisoners, nine of whom eventually dangled from Parker's gallows.

'That's fifty of my original two hundred officers dead. It's not good enough, Mr Thomas. You showed extreme recklessness and a lack of caution and concern for these officers' safety. It is a sad day for all,' Judge Parker intoned at the inquiry. 'Saddest, perhaps, for the widow of Marshal Jim Guy, a brave and dedicated officer.'

'I misjudged the situation, sir,' Heck said. 'I can only express my deepest regrets.'

The four Fort Smith newspapers jumped on the story. THE MARSHAL'S SHAME, was one banner headline, and another, FOUR GOOD OFFICERS DEAD DUE TO ONE GUNHAPPY LAWMAN.

'I led the attack. I gotta take the criticism.' Heck shrugged and tugged at his danglers when Zeke said he thought the papers unfair. But he could see the older man was disturbed. A collection was taken up for the widow, but the deputies were not wealthy and the townspeople soon forgot the deaths of men who were attending to their safety.

They only raised $230.

When Heck presented it to the widow after the funeral ceremonies of the officers, Mrs Guy murmured her thanks and said, 'I guess I'll have to start taking in washing.'

Spring was in the air, however, and, as the poet said, 'a young man's fancy lightly turns to love.'

Zeke was no exception. He picked a posy of spring flowers and sought out Pearl at the Horse's Leg saloon. He frowned to see her waltzing happily around in the arms of a notorious cardsharp and gambler, Xerxes Beauregard. And she pouted peevishly when Zeke tried to present his by now wilted posy to her. 'I'm busy. Cain't you see?' she said.

'Aincha missed me?' Zeke wailed.

'Missed you? Why should I miss you?' Pearl turned to smirk at her dance companion, hanging onto him. 'I only had a couple of five-cent spins with this person and he seems to think he owns me.'

'But you said,' Zeke stuttered. 'I've spoke to your ma. She says . . . she says it's OK if we git wed.'

'Yes, I've spoken to her, too. You're both out of your minds if you think I would want to wed you.'

49

Pearl was wearing an even sillier hat, a felt bluebird perched amid a ruffle of green silk, and she spun away hanging to Beauregard, a snappy dancer in his polished boots, tight pants, blue frockcoat, flowered cravat and canary-yellow waistcoat. His black hair was greased back and his teeth flashed beneath a pencil moustache as he executed some nifty steps.

Suddenly Zeke caught hold of him by the shoulder. 'Excuse me, pal, I'm cutting in.'

'Oh no, you're not, you clodhopper,' Pearl squealed, hanging onto the gambler. 'X, tell this person to cease bothering me.'

'Yeah, push off, pisshead, you're making a fool of yourself,' Beauregard snarled. 'Me and this young lady are engaged.'

'The cheek!' Pearl exclaimed, setting them spinning again to the discordant harmonies pumped out from the podium. 'The nerve! That down-at-heel hick thinking I would want to marry him.'

Zeke went over to the bar and ordered a beer. As he took a deep draught to quell his anger he saw his reflection in the mirror behind the shelf of bottles and guessed Pearl had a point. A stupid young greenhorn – at least, when it came to this love game – with a head of spiky hedgehog hair, a loose bandanna, and his once immaculate Sunday suit now torn and dusty, the tight trousers concertinaed all the way down to his unpolished boots. Certainly the opposite to that beau Pearl had such a regard for. He could see her sailing past now, gazing adoringly into his eyes. No doubt their financial situation was the opposite, too. All Zeke owned was his horse and guns and the five crumpled greenbacks in his pocket. He had left his guns and hat on a hook in the hallway and hoped the gambler had done the same for all of a sudden he was impelled by a terrible jealousy, certain that folks were sniggering and pointing at him.

'Excuse me, X,' he snapped out, catching hold of his shoulder again and, as the gambler turned from Pearl, smashed his right fist into his carefully shaven jaw to send him back-pedalling across the dance floor and tumbling onto a card table. 'You're officially an ex. Stay away from my gal.'

Pearl screamed and rat-tatted her own fists at Zeke's head. 'You leave him alone, you brute. Mister Beauregard has been very good to me. You think I want to stay in this rathole all my life? He's taking me to N'awleans.'

'Stay outa this.' Zeke shrugged her off as Xerxes

51

climbed to his feet, grabbed a bottle, cracked it on a table, ran across and aimed it at his head.

The youngster ducked as it whistled back and forth. If the jagged edges had connected they sure would have ruined his good looks.

The young deputy hurled himself at the gambler knocking him to the floorboards, struggling to get hold of his arm and twist the bottle from his grasp. When he did so he smashed him again and again across the jaw with his fist. 'Had enough?' he panted.

'Get lost!' Beauregard kneed him in the groin, rolling him over his head. First up, he tried to stomp on the youngster. Glad he ain't wearing spurs, Zeke thought, as a boot-heel caught his cheek. He grabbed X's ankle, twisted hard and sent him spinning. The crowd picked him up and threw him back in the ring. 'Go on,' a man roared. 'Finish him!'

Both men now adopted pugilist poses, dancing around each other. Bigger and heavier, the gambler smacked Zeke hard on the nose and lips, making his eyes water. The saloon had erupted into a bedlam of noise but Zeke wasn't sure who they were shouting for. Nor where his opponent was as heavy blows thudded into him.

His eyes cleared and he hurled a series of desperate haymakers in X's direction. The last one knocked the gambler to the floor again. Zeke slipped and joined him as Beauregard tried to grab the broken bottle.

Zeke scrambled to his feet, kicking the bottle away. 'You lowdown, twistin' cardsharp. Go back to your roulette wheel. You ain't no good to her. I've told ya – she's *my* gal.'

'You think so?' Beauregard climbed groggily to his feet, too, and brushed down his now not so immaculate frockcoat. But he had another trick up his sleeve. A two-shot derringer, silver-enscrolled and dainty, which suddenly appeared between his manicured fingers. 'That's where you've made a mistake, cowboy. Nobody gets away with insulting a Southern gentleman.'

'Except me,' Pearl said from behind him. The gambler's finger was on the trigger and he undoubtedly intended to shoot down his upstart opponent. Pearl smiled as she raised a chair in her hands and smashed him across the back of his head, felling him. 'Sorry, X, but I couldn't let you do that.'

Zeke picked up the derringer, examined its two-inch barrel. 'Whoo! What is this toy? Is it real?'

He accidentally pressed the trigger and a bullet sped out almost parting the barkeep's hair and smashing the mirror behind the shelf. 'Yeah, I guess it must be.'

'Beau will pay for the damages,' Pearl squealed, grabbing hold of Zeke's arm. 'Come on, let's git outa here, you numbskull.'

He awoke sprawled on soft bales of cotton in Frizzell's open-fronted loft. His ribs ached, and his nose was sore, his lips were puffed up and one eye was half-closed, but he had Pearl nestled beside him so he felt fine. 'Goodness! Where are we?' she cooed, as she opened her eyes. 'What am I doin'?' The rays of the rising sun were flickering off the river into the cotton factor's warehouse. 'I gotta get outa here.'

'You seemed to think it was a good idea last night.' Zeke gave her a squeeze and kissed her chubby cheek. 'Shall we—?'

'No, we shan't! What a sight I must look. Oh, dear, where's my new hat?'

'Over there where you tossed it. It's fine. You're gorgeous, Pearl. Won't it be great when we're married? We'll be able to cuddle up like this every night.'

'Will we?' Pearl sat up, raking her mop of ringlets with her fingers. 'I ain't so sure about that. Golly gee, just look at your eye. Well, you can't, can you? You've got a real shiner, Zeke.'

'Yeah, it feels like it.' He grinned, ruefully. 'But it was worth it.'

'Oh, my hero!' she sang out, hooking her strong little arm around his neck. 'How sweet of you to fight over me.'

He winced in her headlock and muttered, 'You stay away from that Beauregard from now on. He's damn lucky I didn't arrest him for carrying a concealed weapon.'

'Aw, X is OK. He don't give a damn about me, I know that. Still, ain't you men all the same, just after a gal for one thing?'

'I've told ya, Pearl, I wanna do the honourable thing.'

'Huh! What you wanna marry into a rough old fambly like mine for? You know my daddy's Cole Younger? Or so Ma says.'

'Yup.' Most folks knew Cole rode with Jesse James and the Quantrill Raiders in the war, that for ten years after he had carried on killing and raiding with the James gang until at Northfield, Minnesota, a bank heist was disastrous, the citizens

55

fought back, many died, and Cole was captured. 'He got life, didn't he?'

'That's right. So I've never really met my daddy. In the early days Ma was his gun moll down in Texas. That's when she started to go wrong.' Pearl turned her bright blue eyes on him. 'Oops, I was forgettin', you're a deputy. 'Course, she's turned over a new leaf. Pure as the driven snow these days!'

'It don't matter to me, Pearl. It don't mean you gotta be bad just 'cause she is. Why don't we go and visit them and let them Starrs know you don't intend to follow in their footsteps?'

'You don't believe in bad blood?'

' 'Course not. You seem a nice sweet gal to me.'

'Huh.' Pearl gave a wistful smile. 'If only.'

'Mind you, that brother of yourn seems a bit weird.'

'Ed? Yes, weird ain't the word. I think that's because Ma mollycoddles him. Maybe more 'n that.' The girl stared into her silent memories, jagging back her lips with a look of disgust. 'That boy, he was always watching me dress, trying to . . . you know what.'

'Your brother?'

'Yes, he's weird all right. The whole family is.

That's why I got away. It gets a bit oppressive out there. Still, why am I tellin' you this?' Pearl stood up, hitched her skirt, straightened her blouse, brushed bits of cotton from her hair. 'I gotta go see Molly an' Vera.'

'Who are they?' Zeke asked, alarmed he might lose her.

'You know. Them two I was with. My gal pals.'

Just then Heck Thomas strode into the quayside warehouse. 'So, here y'are,' he shouted. 'I mighta known. It's time to be moving, Sonny Jim. Judge's orders. We're going after 'em.'

'Who? The Lees?' Zeke jumped up in some confusion, buttoning his trousers, buckling his gunbelt. 'Where'd I put my carbine?'

'Christ's sake, cowboy! Pull yourself together. You don't leave your Winchester for anyone to snaffle, do ya? What the hell you been up to? You look like you done been in a prize fight.'

'Yeah, well, I was, sorta,' Zeke mumbled, finding the carbine. 'What's the big hurry, Heck?'

'Four men dead. The biggest loss our outfit's ever suffered. *That's* the big hurry. The judge says we gotta go back and bring those bastards in. So move it, mister. It's just you and me on our own this time.'

Zeke regarded Pearl anxiously. She was fitting her hat with a long pin into her curls. 'What *you* gonna do?'

'Aw, 'she shrugged. 'Don't worry about me. I'll be around.'

'Well,' he touched her arm, uncertainly, 'don't—'

'What the hell!' Heck Thomas roared. 'Aincha had enough of that doxy's honeypot for one night? Go get your hoss, Deputy Jones. At the double. That's an order. Or—'

'I'm going,' Zeke yelled, jumping from the loft, jerking his hat down over his nose, stumbling away and out of the stable door. 'So long, Pearl.'

The immaculately attired marshal stroked his heavy walrus moustache and glanced up at the girl. 'Seems like the boy's infatuated, don't it?' He jabbed a forefinger at her. 'You just be careful what you're up to.'

Pearl gave a shrug and a wistful smile. 'I allus am, Marshal. You know that.'

SEVEN

Pink Lee and his brother, Jim, led a string of horses through an early morning haze of misty rain towards a smell of woodsmoke. They spied it drifting from the chimney of a solid sod building, grass sprouting from its flat roof. There was a rough pole corral alongside a wooden barn so they herded the stolen beasts inside and secured them. A notice tacked to the barn proclaimed, '*Horses shod $3 a foot.*' They could hear the clang of hammer on anvil from inside. But their interest lay in the cabin. They hitched their own mustangs to a rail outside and, their heavy rifles in hand, kicked open the wooden door.

'Hello there,' the saloon-keeper, Tom Mahoney called. 'What is it you'd be wanting?'

The brothers ducked through the low doorway and peered at the assorted collection of booze hoisters hunched on wooden benches in the smoky gloom. None appeared to present any threat so they laid their rifles aside. 'What the hell ya think we want?' Pink growled. 'A sup of your moonshine.'

They had penetrated deep south into the Chickasaw nation, a wilderness of forests, lakes and streams, aware that there was a price on their heads, which only increased their callous disregard for life or property.

Pink stomped his boots on the solid earth, for the cabin had no raised flooring, and flapped his arms in his sodden topcoat to bring back the circulation after a night of sleeping rough. He warmed his backside at the log fire and balefully regarded the assorted sots. 'Looks like you varmints start your drinkin' early,' he muttered. 'Or have ya bin at it all night?'

Two Texans in range clothes, spurred boots, leather chaps, colourful shirts and bandannas, turned to them and one drawled, 'We'd like the chance, my friend, but some of us have work to do.'

'Get *him*,' Jim snorted. 'Goody Two Shoes.'

60

Mahoney had filled two clay pots with whiskey from the barrel. He plonked them down on his bar, a plank resting on two barrels, and chimed in, 'Dat'll be a quarter, gents.'

'A quarter? Bit pricey, aincha?' Pink grabbed his pot and guzzled greedily before coughing and retching. 'Christ! What you put in this? A dead rat?'

'Dat's funny. How did you guess?' Mahoney smiled sweetly. 'It adds to the flavour, don't it?'

There were several other seedy-looking Anglos in drab outfits, and an Indian, more colourful in a blanket coat and beaded necklace, his hair hung about his shoulders, plus a sturdy black fellow sitting in the shadows, all of whom burst into guffaws at Pink's coughing fit.

'Us Lees don't like being the butt of folks' humour.' Jim patted the butt of the revolver in his belt. 'You boys better remember that.'

The men quickly ceased cackling and the wide grin of the black man disappeared like a lamp being doused. 'It's so dark in here I didn't see you sittin' in the shadows,' Jim Lee leered, insultingly, at the man, but he made no reply. 'Aw, I'm only jokin'. Pull yerself together, Pink, and pay the man.'

Mahoney caught the quarter that went spinning towards him. He had his own still in the woods where he made his moonshine. 'I'm the one who's taking the risk,' he said. 'I'm the one who goes to jail if the deputies come calling.'

'Aw, don't talk about *them*.' Pink wiped his rheumy eyes and put out his pot for a refill. '*They* ain't anybody's favourite customers.'

'Jasus an' Mary!' Mahoney yelped. 'God forbid!'

'Why?' Jim asked. 'You seen any sign of any?'

'No,' Mahoney replied. 'T'anks to the Lord they don't much bother us in this outa-the-way corner.'

'Good. In that case,' Jim announced, 'anybody int'rested in buying some horseflesh? We got 'em outside.'

The Texan rancher, Andy Roff, looked over. 'I might be. I'm short of stock.' He got to his feet. 'Let's take a look, Jim.'

'Howja know my name's Jim?' Lee asked.

'I'm talking to my brother, he's Jim, too.'

'Duh. Ain't that funny?' The near-toothless Pink started giggling idiotically, and mock-punched his brother. 'He got a brudder Jim, just like me.'

'Yuh, I hope he ain't as stoopid as you. Come on.' Jim Lee led them out to the corral where the two ranchers dubiously inspected the herd of a dozen. They were runty, thick-haired Indian ponies. 'Two hundred dollars for the lot. You won't get a better bargain than that, gents.'

'Where'd you get these? You got a bill of sale?'

'Up north some place. Bill of sale? Hey, Pink, what'd you do with it?'

'You had it. Not me. You got my word.' The hillbilly grinned at them, gummily. 'Them hosses were honestly obtained.'

'That's very doubtful,' Jim Roff opined. 'What you think, Andy?'

Andy shrugged. 'Anybody comes lookin' we'll have to give 'em up,' he said. 'So fifty's the most we'll risk.'

'Fifty,' Pink wailed. 'Aw, OK, divvy up.'

He held out a dirt-engrained hand. Andy Roff took a leather pouch from his pocket and paid him in two gold twenty-dollar cartwheels, and ten in silver.

Pink spat on the cash and stuffed it in his topcoat pocket. He turned back to the cabin. 'C'mon, Jim. I got a terrible thirst.'

The Roff brothers watched them go. 'I don't like it,' Andy remarked, 'but we need the stock. C'mon, let's get these critters back to the ranch.'

Back in the bar Jim Lee tested one of the gold

pieces with his last remaining tooth. 'Real enough,' he said, slapping it down. 'You keep the whiskey comin', mister. We're plannin' on gittin' drunk as skunks. Where's them two come from?'

'They got a place ten miles down Eagle Creek trail.'

'They allus pay in gold?'

'Gen'rally. There ain't no banks around here,' Mahoney mused. 'It wouldn't surprise me if they had a pot of it hidden in their backyard.'

'You don't say?' Jim raised his mug and winked at Pink. 'Some fellas have all the luck, don't they?'

Instead of following the Arkansas River 135 miles upstream to Fort Gibson, Heck Thomas had struck across country south-west, climbing into the high mountains to follow the winding Talimena trail with glorious views for fifty miles or more. The marshal and his deputy gradually descended from the skyline ridge through blackjack hills, quail meadows and dogwood trails. There were waterfalls and deep, clear springs and they travelled light, living off the land mostly.

They had entered Choctaw and Chickasaw territory. But white settlers were poised eyeing this lush land enviously. Many so-called Sooners had

64

defied the government and moved in, building log cabins, marking out farms with pole fences, raising cattle and crops. Some were turned back by federal troops, a blind eye turned to the incursions of others. There was a string of all-black towns settled by 70,000 freed slaves of the Cherokee, while the native Indians struggled to hang on to their land and customs. Once they had exported cattle, tobacco and cotton but jealousy of their tax-free status had hit that trade. Everywhere white folk were clamouring to have the land thrown open and within a decade would come the first of the great land races.

But, mostly, the country was still wild and beautiful and Zeke revelled in riding his Appaloosa forty or fifty miles a day behind Heck's quarter horse. He marvelled at how the marshal led the way, skirting steep hillsides, crossing rivers and a varied terrain as if sensing the way. The partnership between horse and man became ever more apparent as they allowed their mounts to pick their own paths.

The evenings were drawing out and the early May sunshine made his spirits soar. Sometimes they would set lines with grasshopper bait to catch speckled trout, at others shoot quail, jack-rabbits or partridge to clean and cook over their fires. Their biggest danger so far was from snakes or mountain lions. They slept easy under the stars but kept their carbines close at hand. A man never knew who might come sneaking up, a horse-thieving Indian or white cut-throat.

Heck was a man of few words but one night around their camp-fire asked, 'Where'd you get that spotted hoss of yourn?'

Zeke looked across at the Appaloosa, contentedly cropping the grass beside the quarter horse, and replied, 'My pa give him to me when I left home.'

'Where would that have been?'

'We hail from Kentucky, but after the war there was so much bitterness my folks crossed the Mississippi and settled in Arkansas. My daddy traded horses. Good ones. He specialized in these Appaloosas. They're much in demand by rodeos and circuses. Did you know that, like snowflakes, no two Appaloosas have the same coat pattern?'

'No, I didn't know that. So why didn't you stay and work in the family business?'

'I got three brothers and two sisters. There weren't room or the profit in it for me.' Zeke scratched at his blond thatch and grinned.

'Anyhow I fancied seeing the world.'

'So, what prompted you to come to Fort Smith and join the service? You got romantic ideas about doing good and cleaning out the bad guys? Maybe you thought it'd be like King Arthur and his Round Table?'

'Yeah, well, maybe I saw myself more like that fella d'Artagnan and the three musketeers.' Zeke lovingly polished the blued six-inch barrel of his double action Smith & Wesson, raised it and pretend fired. 'But with a six-gun not a sword.'

'Well, one thing's for sure, it ain't much like that. It's a hard, ugly profession you've chose.' Heck sighed and filled his pipe as he leaned back against his saddle. 'And you ain't got much hope of gittin' rich. You'll be lucky to save enough to cover your own funeral.'

'So, why'd you stick with it, Heck?'

Thomas smiled, nonplussed. 'I'm danged if I know.'

They had already been travelling for several weeks with no sightings of the Lees. When the weather broke and Zeke sat on a rock one night in his rubberized cape, rainwater tipping off his hat brim, he asked, despondently, 'How long we gonna go on searching for these two? We ain't had no sign of 'em.'

Heck looked at him and gritted out, 'When a United States Marshal goes on the trail of a criminal there ain't no giving up, boy, no going back.'

But in a small town called Poteau, they heard from a man called Chouteau, whose family had run trading stores in the Nations since 1796, that a Choctaw Indian had been killed by two thugs closely resembling the Lees, who had got away with a dozen horses. 'It's them,' Heck said. 'It's all them killers got the imagination for, thievin' hosses.'

Soon they would hear that even worse had occurred.

EIGHT

The Roff brothers' small ranch in the heart of the Ouachita forest was about as lonesome as lonesome could get. Owls hooted lugubriously as Andy locked up the barn. Out in the blackness of the night there was the shrill agonized cry of some creature as a predator pounced.

'Sounds like that puma's on the prowl,' Andy said, as he went into the ranch-house kitchen. 'Hope he leaves our foals alone.'

His wife, Ice, a full-blood Chickasaw, in a white buckskin dress, her hair, held by a beaded filet around her brow, tumbling to her shoulders like a black, shimmering waterfall, was cooking at the stove, preparing their evening meal.

Jim was sat at the table, tamping his pipe. 'I'll

69

take a look around for him later tonight,' he muttered.

Their older brother, Alva, had done well for himself as a cattleman in Texas, but finding a piece of land free for homesteaders was not easy these days. So Andy and Jim had gone north of the Red River to try their luck in the Nations. And lucky Andy had been in meeting Ice Along the Edge of the Stream Melting in the Springtime Sun, to give her her full name. Not only was she slim and comely, she was a chief's daughter and being married to her, gave him legal right to settle their ten-mile strip of valley amid the wooded hills. They had worked hard and built up a decent herd and soon it would be time to trail them north to the markets of Kansas. All in all life was pretty good up until that moment. How suddenly it could change.

Their hound dog growled at the sound of horses' hoofs outside. 'Who's that?' Jim wondered, picking up his shotgun and going outside. 'What can I do for you?' he called to a rider on a bay mare.

Pink Lee raised his revolver and blasted the Texan to extinction from point blank-range. When the hound leapt snarling at him he shot him dead, too. He grinned at the bodies of man and dog bleeding and twitching their last on the ground. 'Dat was a silly question. What's he think we want?'

Inside the wooden house, Andy had pulled out his own revolver, beckoning to Ice to stay where she was. 'What the hell's going on?'

Suddenly the window of the wall behind was smashed and Jim Lee poked his rifle through. 'Freeze!' he shouted. 'Don't make a move.' He cackled with laughter as Andy obeyed him. 'OK, Pink,' he yelled. 'Safe to come in. He knows better than try anythang.'

The runty little Pink, in his floppy-brimmed hat and filthy garments stepped into the kitchen, disarmed Andy, then looked lecherously at the Indian girl. 'Waal, look at what we got here!' He ducked as Ice hurled a big kitchen knife at him and it thudded into the door. 'Ye'll have to do better than that, darlin'.'

'What do you want?' Andy demanded, keeping his hands raised.

'Anudder one asking stoopid questions.' Pink cracked him across the temple with his pistol butt and Andy went down on one knee. 'What you think we want? All that gold you got hid.'

'What gold?' Andy gasped. 'We ain't got no gold. Only what's in my pocket. Take that and go.'

Jim had climbed through the smashed window. 'We go when we get that pot of gold. We ain't got time to argue. First we'll burn the squaw, then we'll rape her. You wanna watch or you wanna talk? Just give us the gold. Thass all you gotta do.'

'Leave her alone, 'Andy gritted out. 'You touch her and it'll be the last thing you do.'

'Oh, yuh?' Jim grabbed a handful of Ice's hair and pulled it tight, hauling her into him. 'I could git a hundred dollars for this fine scalp.'

He screamed as Ice gripped the handle of the stewpot on the tin stove, swinging it at him. The scalding contents hit him in the face and chest and Jim Lee released her, staggering about, wiping at his eyes. 'You bitch . . . you'll pay for this.'

Pink had now caught Andy by his hair and had his revolver pressed hard to his temple. 'Hold it,' he shouted. 'Or he's a dead man.'

'Please, mister. Don't kill him,' Ice pleaded. 'Do what you like to me.'

Jim was cursing, screaming and raging like a tormented bear. His matted beard and hair had taken the worst of the hot stew but he was livid. 'Right, you asked fer it, you witch's spawn.' He gripped hold of her arm and pressed her hand hard down on the hot stove.

72

'All right!' Ice's scream cut through Andy Roff's heart like an icicle. 'Leave her. I'll tell you. You can have the gold. I'll show you.'

With Pink hanging onto him he staggered over to the chimney breast and pointed to a loose brick. 'There.'

Jim cackled with glee as he removed it, put in his hand and brought out a tin box. He pulled open the lid to reveal a horde of gold and silver dollar pieces. 'Waal, whadda ya know? The Lord's lookin'down on us this day.'

'There's near on two thousand dollars. Take it and go,' Andy gritted out. 'You won't hear no more from us.'

'No, we sure won't,' Pink grinned, shoving him towards the girl. 'Dat's a fact.' He raised his pistol and the explosions crashed out. . . .

Alva Roff looked the typical Texan, like a Longhorn, long-legged, narrow-hipped, lean, mean and horny. When he heard the news of his brothers' deaths he left his ranch in Gainesville and rode north with a couple of his cowhands into the Nations. They headed from Octavia up the Big Eagle Creek and along Eagle Fork Creek to the ranch, a sad scene of desolation.

He was hammering wooden crosses into the graves down by the riverside when he saw two men ride in. One he mistook for a preacher in his black suit, clean shaven but for a moustache, his face shaded by the wide brim of his new black, bowl-shaped hat, until he spotted the US marshal's badge on his lapel. His sidekick looked more like a cowboy with a goofy grin beneath tousled blond hair.

'How did they go?' Heck Thomas asked, after expressing his regrets.

'Both boys shot at close range,' Alva replied, explaining what he had gleaned of the robbery.

'I heard there was an Indian gal involved.'

'Andy's wife, Ice. They were wed according to tribal law so now she's the legal owner of this homestead. She ain't said what she plans to do. Maybe go back to her tribe, maybe stay, I dunno. A coupla my boys are lookin' after the place for her for the time being. Maybe me and her'll go into partnership.'

'Where is she?'

'In the kitchen. Go easy on her, Marshal. The gal's been hurt bad,' Alva said. 'I guess she's still in a state of shock.'

They found the Indian girl in the ranch-house

kitchen sitting in a rocker, wrapped in blankets, her right hand swathed in bandage. Zeke was struck by her calm beauty, the glow of her dark eyes as she contemplated them.

'Are you able to give us the facts, ma'am?' the marshal asked.

For moments she gazed at them with a haughty imperiousness as if wondering what these white men, with their guns, who had invaded and despoiled the lands, corrupted her people, wanted with her now. 'They killed my man and his brother. Didn't give them a chance. They stole their gold.'

'What about you?' Zeke prompted, gently.

'Me? They burned me on that stove. They beat me, raped me, stabbed me, left me for dead. When they had gone I lay in the icy river, washed my wounds clean.'

When Alva Roff joined them in the kitchen the marshal remarked, 'Sounds like the Lees, sure enough. It's got all their hallmarks.'

'I guess Ice is lucky to be alive,' Alva drawled, as he boiled coffee for them all.

'Yes,' the young woman said, 'at least they left me my hair. Kind of them.'

There was a bit of an awkward silence, then Zeke was prompted to blurt out, 'I'm glad they did, ma'am. You sure got lovely black tresses.'

Ice regarded him as if he were an idiot, then for the first time in days smiled, faintly. 'Thank you for saying so.' She met his sunny blue eyes. 'What do they call *you*?'

'Zeke. Yeah, I know, I got lovely *yeller* hair. Or so my mammy used to tell me.' Some message passed silently between him and the Indian girl but he was not sure what. 'If it's any consolation we are gonna catch them for ya, ma'am. They kilt four of our men.'

'I sure hope you do,' Alva Roff exclaimed. 'I've put up a reward of two thousand five hundred dollars on their heads, dead or alive. You bring 'em to me in Gainesville the reward's yourn.'

'We ain't really s'posed to do that,' Thomas said. 'We're s'posed to take 'em back to Fort Smith.'

'How much will you get for that?'

'Two dollars arrest fee and expenses. We ain't doin' this for the cash, Mr Roff.'

'More fool you. Make an exception this time,' the Texan said, as the two lawmen got up to leave. 'Whatever, the best of luck. Watch out for those varmints.'

'Thanks,' Thomas said. 'Don't worry. We will.'

NINE

Marshal Thomas was surprised to see a four-mule stagecoach, overloaded with passengers, eight on top and six more inside, rocking along up the Texas Trail from Boggy Depot on the Red River. 'Didn't know you were still operating this line,' he shouted to the gnarled and hairy driver, Too Morrow, when he hauled in in a cloud of dust.

'We're back in operation, San Antone to Fort Smith,' Too yelled. 'Two of Butterfield's partners, Mr Fargo and Mr Wells, have taken over. 'Course it ain't like the old times.'

In his younger days Too Morrow had faced hostile Indians driving the Butterfield Overland Mail, the only transcontinental connection from the Mississippi to the west coast. But the building of the Central Pacific railroad had put paid to that.

'You seen any sign of them two murdering scallawags, the Lee brothers?'

'Nope.' The stage guard brandished his shotgun. 'If we had we'd be claimin' the reward.'

'If you were still alive,' Heck muttered, taking a notepad and pencil from his suit pocket. He scribbled a brief message. 'Can you give this to Judge Parker? Or better still, just tell him we're still on their trail and we ain't giving up.'

'Sure thang, boys.' Too cracked his whip over the mules' ears and the coach went lumbering on its way. 'Good hunting.'

'If they ain't gawn south,' Heck drawled, 'I figure they've high-tailed it back north. My hunch is we may find 'em roosting in one of their old haunts.'

'If I were them and had all that cash,' Zeke opined, 'I'd be heading for California or the Mex border. That's if I was a badman.'

'Aw, they ain't got the sense for that. At least, I hope not.'

The two lawmen had called in at Mahoney's cabin in the forest near Eagle's Nest and elicited that the Lees had passed back through there. So that, too, seemed to confirm they were going north-west rather than south.

Eager to please, Mahoney had stuttered out, 'They was here before. Sold some ponies to the Roff brothers. They was paid in gold. My opinion is that's why the Lees followed 'em. A terrible thing it was, indeed.'

'You're lucky, Mr Mahoney. We ought to take you in. But, quite frankly, we ain't got time. My deputy's gonna have to destroy all your stock.'

'Oh, holy mercy, 'Mahoney wailed, as Zeke commenced to stove in all his barrels of moonshine. 'That's cruel.'

Heck sampled a drop of the fiery liquid and spat it out. 'I'm warning you, we'll be back this way again. If we find any of this ruckus juice here you'll be serving a year in the penitentiary, I can assure you.'

'Oh, no, sir, I'll never brew anudder drop,' Mahoney cried. 'I've learned my lesson. Thank you, sir. You can trust me.'

'Yeah, like I'd trust a scorpion,' Heck had remarked, as they went back out to their horses.

It was obvious the Lees were riding hard and fast and the two lawmen pressed on after them. Broken Bow . . . Corinne . . . Antlers . . . and on north into the mountains; Dunbay . . . Clayton . . .

it was the same answer: the Lees had been and gone.

'They come through here like dose of salts,' the half-Indian owner of a low dance hall dive at Yanush told them. 'They chuck gold and silver around like no tomorrow. Them bad wimmin who hang 'round here didn't know what hit 'em.'

'Yeah, I can guess,' Heck Thomas observed, wearily. 'We'll head on up to the Robber's Cave.'

'Where's that?'

'North of here. All kinda badmen been using it as a hideout. They say Belle Starr used to meet up with Jesse James there. But I ain't over optimistic.'

No, the huge cavern in the mountains was deserted, even though there were signs of recent camp-fires. Heck and Zeke made their own camp and stayed a night in its echoing interior. The 18-year-old lay rolled in his blanket watching the eerie shadows flickering on the cave roof, his Winchester snugly between his knees, and his hand on his other weapon as he pined for Pearl. The fires of sex and unrequited love tortured him as he wondered what she would be up to. Did she feel torn apart like him? Or would she have gone back to that skunk Beauregard? His one night in the cotton loft with her had shown him that she obviously had an easy expertise with men. Wonderful as that night had been, it tormented him to imagine her tricks with other . . . no, she would not, surely?

And then, when his lascivious imaginings of Pearl had passed, he found himself thinking of Ice, her dark, molten eyes, her pain which she bore with such disdain. There was something about the Indian girl that made him feel more at peace. Strange, he thought. Surely he couldn't be in love with two girls at one and the same time?

But, as spring days passed into the lushness of summer, Zeke was having the time of his life, riding his horse, swimming in the lakes, sleeping under the stars, proud to be a US deputy marshal, to be learning how to doggedly trail badmen from an expert at the game.

One morning they met a wild-looking fellow in a coonskin cap and buckskins driving a team of ten long-horned oxen pulling his covered wagon and a trail wagon. The man's wife and small daughter were sitting beside him, and a seven-year-old boy walked alongside the lead ox.

'Howdy,' Heck called, raising his hand to halt him. 'I'm a US marshal. What we got here?'

81

'Fox furs, marten, bearskins, beef hides, buff'
robes, blankets, sheep wool, deer skins, tallow,
bees' wax, beaded moccasins and other
embroidered Chickasaw valuables. You name it, we
got it. You sure you're marshals?' He held a rifle
half-aimed at them. 'Can I take a squint at that
badge?'

'Sure, take a look around the back, Zeke.'

The young deputy nudged his Appaloosa
around the wagons, peered through a backflap of
the first one. It was stacked with furs and stuff,
likewise the trailer. Hanging on the back were two
home-made cages, one with a pair of indignant
chickens inside, the other holding two snarling
puma cubs.

'What you gonna do with them li'l mountain
lions?' he asked when he returned. 'Use 'em as
guard dogs?'

'No, I got two of *them*.' The frontiersman
indicated two big elk hounds watching them. 'I'll
sell 'em to a circus.'

Heck was studying a crumpled piece of
parchment he had been presented with and
handed it back. 'Everything's in order, Mr Judd.'

' 'Course it's in order,' Judd replied angrily.
'This licence to trade with the tribes cost me ten

thousand dollars for one year. This gov'ment's no better than cut-throat pirates. It's a damned disgrace. No wonder I'm a poor man.'

'Yeah, well,' Heck muttered, 'we all got our crosses to bear. Carry on, Mr Judd. We'll be on our way.'

'How do you ever get used to the sudden death of your comrades?' Zeke asked one morning. 'I mean I'd only known Big Jim, Josh Abrahams, Bill and Abe for a couple of weeks, but suddenly they're blasted to smithereens. I still can't get used to the idea of 'em gone.'

Marshal Thomas was straddling a fallen tree, a small mirror propped on its bough, using his coffee mug of hot water to get a lather and carefully shaving his jaws with a cut-throat razor. 'Who did your daddy support in the war?'

'The Union. Why? It was neighbour split against neighbour on the Kentucky border, brother against brother. There were some terrible things done. Or so he said. That's why he moved out after the peace.'

'Waal, I was raised in Georgia. At ten years old I was taken as regimental drummer boy. I had no idea what was going on 'cept we were fighting for the Southern cause.' Heck spoke in his soft saw-tooth drawl. 'I seen things would make your hair stand on end, Zeke, if it didn't do that already of its own accord. Cotton gins and farmsteads burning; hogs feeding on the dead; corpses piled up like cordwood; ambulance tents with piles of bloody legs and arms outside. Pitiful, starving men shot for cowardice; screaming horses slaughtered as they charged into the mouths of cannons. A terrible conflagration it was. That was my baptism of fire. I became used to the sight and sound of death at an early age.'

'Jeeze!' Zeke shook his head in awe. 'That don't sound nice. But it seems odd to me that now you work as a Union law officer. I mean, so many of your ol' Southern boys seem to be still fightin' the war.'

The marshal took a pair of scissors from his wallet and trimmed his sideburns and moustache. Even when living rough he tried to look neat. 'I took the oath of allegiance. We're one nation now. We've got to forget the bitterness of the past. I happen to believe in law and order. That's what I've fought for all my life. I was a railroad detective in Texas, foiled Sam Bass's gang when they tried to rob us of twenty thousand dollars. It was natural for me to become a US deputy, and I was proud when I was promoted marshal. I guess it's just who I am.'

Zeke pondered this as he washed their tin plates in a stream and packed his saddle-bags ready to move off. 'You think we're gettin' near?'

'I've a hunch we are. All the information leads this way. A trail of misspent gold.' The marshal crouched to splash his face in the stream and wiped his chin with his bandanna. 'You figure you're up to this, Zeke? We cain't afford any mistakes. I don't want no more of my men dead.'

'I'm ready,' Zeke replied, sticking his Winchester into the saddle boot. 'Ready as I'll ever be.'

'If we meet these boys I ain't gonna play it by the usual rules.' Thomas gathered his reins, put a foot in his bentwood stirrup and swung aboard the deep-chested quarter horse. 'I'll give 'em one warning. That's all they get. Then we start shooting. OK?'

'OK.' Zeke leapt onto the Appaloosa. 'I said I'm ready, Marshal.'

TEN

Cut-throat Crossroads, the locals called it, and the crossing of two trails in a dark forest of cedars was aptly named. Gloomy and misty after a thunderstorm, the great trees towered some 150 feet tall. In the crossroads clearing were two log shacks. One acted as a way station for a stage line, with a corral holding fresh horses outside. The other sold vittles, blankets, clothing and general goods and, if there was any available, bootleg hooch.

Heck Thomas drew in his horse in the safety of the trees and regarded the small trading post. 'Maybe this is a lot to ask, Zeke, but how about if you go in first on your own and get the lie of the land? You're new and unknown in the service.

Most of whoever's in there will recognize me immediately.'

'Sure.' Zeke couldn't disguise the concern in his voice. 'I don't mind. I'll do that.'

'Good. Just put your hoss in that corral. Take off your badge. Leave your Winchester. Just wander across like you're some drifting cowboy, ain't got a care in the world.'

'Right.'

'Zeke! Watch your back. Get a corner spot. There's likely to be a ripe selection of rapscallions in there. I'll jine you exactly ten minutes after you go in. Be ready to start shooting. Good luck, son.'

Zeke nudged his mount forward. His mouth had gone exceedingly dry and a sudden shiver ran up his spine. 'It looks like this is it,' he muttered. 'Now or never. Aw, well, I've had a good life. It's gotta end sometime.'

Zeke loose-hitched the Appaloosa to the corral fence, glanced in the staging post. Just a couple of would-be passengers waiting glumly with their baggage. He strolled across the trail to the trading store. He guessed he looked beat-up enough to pass as any prairie rat, his hair grown long over his nose and the back of his neck, a trickle of blond fuzz, the beginnings of a youthful beard on his face. He loosened the Smith & Wesson in its greased holster pig-stringed to his thigh, and creaked open a wooden door, stepping inside.

A big, black-bearded man was behind a counter checking shelves of clothing. He turned to glower at Zeke. 'Yeah?'

'Any chance of some hot vittles?' Zeke asked. 'A drink?'

'You on your own?'

'Yep. I'm headin' home to Texas.'

The big man nodded to an adjoining room. 'You're in luck. Just had a delivery. There's a pot of Mulligatawny on the stove. Help yourself.'

Zeke's nostrils immediately smelt liquor as he stepped into the low-roofed room, murky with woodsmoke. He also immediately recognized the stunted, toothless Pink Lee from his description.

'Howdy, y'all,' he called, putting on his goofiest of grins and a southern drawl. He removed the lid of the stewpot on a tin stove. 'Smells good,' he said.

There were four other men present who dropped silent and regarded him balefully. One, in a filthy topcoat and floppy-brimmed hat, he took for Pink's brother, Jim. He was sitting on an upturned barrel, a bottle of rum half-raised to his mouth. A ripple of red scalded flesh ran down from his temple to his fleshy cheek.

'Who the hell are *you*?' he said.

'Zeke Williams. Been on a cattle drive up to Kansas. On my way home, poorer and wiser. Pleased to meetcha'll. What's that you're drinkin', mister? Any chance of a belly-warmer?'

A scurvy-faced *hombre* was sitting alongside Jim, his long legs, in buckskin pants and boots, stuck out before him. He looked like a full-blood Indian, wearing Anglo-clothes of a colourful shirt and neckerchief, his hair cut shortish but hanging over his brow. There was menace in his muddy eyes. 'How come you ride alone?' he growled. 'That ain't wise.'

'My *compadre* got drowned in the Cimarron. His pony jest went down under him. Sank like a stone.'

'Too bad.' A Mexican in tight velvet costume and a sombrero had one boot up warming at the stove as he leaned back against the log wall. 'Why didn't you throw heem a rope?'

'He couldn't swim. Went down with the pony. Disappeared. Never saw 'em again. Weird, huh?'

'It's you who's weird,' Pink giggled. 'You come in here tellin' us some cock 'n' bull story. Who *are* you, mister?'

'I ain't nobody.' Zeke felt like the deputy's badge was burning a hole in his pocket. The seconds seemed to crawl by. 'Jest a cowboy, thassal. Aw, c'mon, boys. Aincha got a drop to spare?'

There was a pile of bedding in a dark corner and the deputy suddenly noticed a chubby Indian woman sprawled there. Her dark face was sullen under a mess of black hair. He grinned. 'Hey, is she on the menu, too? Ain't had a drink or a gal in days.'

'Cheeky li'l gofer, ain't he?' the other man, standing behind Pink, his face shadowed by a Stetson, opined. 'Aw, go on, Ned, give him a bottle. Let's watch him git drunk.'

'You got any cash, cowboy?' the long-legged Ned enquired. 'Three dollars a bottle.'

Ned Christie! The outlaw! flashed through the deputy's mind.

'Let's see.' Zeke dug into his pocket and produced what change he had. 'I got two fifty. No, here's another dime.'

He plonked the cash on the barrel top and Ned reached back into a corner and produced a bottle of rum. 'You're lucky. Ain't much left. Sells like hotcakes.'

90

Zeke jerked out the cork with his teeth and took a sup of the musty liquid. 'Whoo-ee!' he yelled. 'The real McCoy.'

How long, he wondered, before Heck burst in? He needed to get behind these curs. Fired by the rum, he howled, 'Hey, how much fer the purty gal?'

Ned gave a throaty chuckle and shouted to the man in the other room, 'He wants to poke your squaw, Gus. How much?'

'Two dollars to him,' the big man boomed back.

'Great Jehosaphat! I ain't paid that much since Abilene.' Zeke found a crumpled five-dollar greenback in his waistcoat pocket and passed it to Ned. 'I need three dollars change.'

'Too bad, kid. We don't give change.'

'In that case, let me at her.' Zeke pushed through them, jumped on the bed, and kneeled over the Indian woman. 'Yee-hoo!' Here I am, honey, have a sup of this. It'll put you in a loving mood.'

'Hark at him,' Jim Lee chortled, taking a bite of his own bottle. 'Kid's sure got an appetite for likker and wimmin.'

Marshal Thomas steeled himself, thumbing back the hammer of his .45 and pushed open the

91

door. He aimed the Colt at the heart of a big, bearded man behind the counter, and with his left hand index finger touched his lips to tell him to stay quiet, then coaxed him with the fingers of that hand to pass over his revolver. He cocked that, too, and stepped into the other room. 'Freeze!' he shouted.

Pink dropped his bottle with surprise. 'Where the hell you spring from?'

As Heck covered them with both revolvers, Jim Lee sprang to his feet and scoffed, 'Didn't figure you for a Two Gun Pete, Marshal. You gonna take us all?'

'You Lees go first, you murdering scumbags,' Thomas said. 'I got no business with you other men. Keep out of this.'

'*Ola, hombre!*' the Mexican sang out, removing his boot from the stove. 'You brave man, *señor*. Or maybe *loco*.'

Zeke had turned from his kneeling position to rest his back against the log wall and gently eased his Smith & Wesson out of the holster, unnoticed in the shadows.

'Yeah, crazy's the word,' Pink hollered. 'Who's he think he is?'

'All of you men,' the marshal gritted out.

'Unbuckle your gunbelts. I ain't telling you twice.'

Suddenly, Pink kicked out at the tin pipe chimney, disconnecting it from the stove and a black cloud of smoke and cinders erupted into the room. Through the murk Zeke saw Jim Lee haul out the revolver from the belt around his topcoat. Zeke fired before Jim had a chance to cock it, the bullet thudding hard into his back.

There was a choking cloud of smoke filling the small cabin as explosions racketed out. Ned Christie raised his revolver and blasted a slug at the marshal, who dodged behind the stove, the bullet whanging off it.

Zeke fired at the shadowy shape of Christie, but his lead ploughed into the unnamed fourth man behind him, who grunted and collapsed over a barrel.

The Mex traded shots with the marshal, but suddenly screamed and fell to the floor groaning, '*Basta!*'

Lead was ricocheting in all directions. Zeke took a pot at Pink but his first shot missed. Before he could fire again he felt a burning pain in his shoulder. The Indian woman had brought a big knife out from under the covers. Before she could stab him again he buffaloed her with his revolver butt. 'Aw, shee-it!' he groaned, at the sight of his own blood.

Pink, out of lead in his six-gun, hauled his slide action Lightning to his shoulder. He fired, demolishing the stove. But Heck Thomas wasn't there any more. He had rolled to a corner and came up aiming both revolvers at the rifle's flash of explosion.

'Damn you, Marshal.' Pink coughed blood, dropped the Lightning and held his shirt front as more gore oozed from his chest. 'I'll see you in Hell.'

'Perhaps.' The marshal got to his feet, warily. 'You'll certainly be there afore me.' He fired once more to settle it and Pink hit the floor hard.

Drifting acrid black powder smoke had increased the gloom of the small room, but peering through it Zeke suddenly saw the big, bearded Gus standing at the door, a double-barrelled shotgun in his hands aimed at the marshal's back.

'Watch out!' he shouted and racketed out the Smith & Wesson's last two slugs. They thudded into the big man before he could squeeze his triggers and his little pink mouth opened with surprise. He back-pedalled and crashed back into his store.

Heck gave a whistle of relief. 'That was a close thing.' He looked around. 'Where's the other one?'

'Ned? Dunno. Musta got out the back door.'

'Sounds like he did.' Heck heard the rattle of hoofbeats and going outside saw Ned Christie galloping fast away through the trees. He warned an ostler and folk who had come from the way-station to stay where they were and returned to the interior of the cabin. 'You OK, Zeke?'

'I think so. This bitch stabbed me. Hurts like hell.'

Heck took a look at him, took off his bandanna to try to staunch the wound. 'It ain't gone too deep. We'll get you patched up. Don't worry, Deputy.' He smiled at Zeke, tousling his hair. 'You done well.'

ELEVEN

The Choctaws' new meeting house was a huge Victorian building of three storeys, its pink granite blocks quarried nearby. Tall, ornate windows on all sides, the Choctaw flag of a bow, a pipe of peace and three arrows flying above, it had cost a total of $50,000 and opened that summer.

'Whoo!' Zeke sat beside Marshal Thomas as he drove a horse and wagon into Tuscahoma. 'What an amazin' sight.'

'Yep,' Heck drawled. 'Some joint. Different to the log house they had here afore.'

The big building seemed to symbolize the US Government's determination to draw the civilized tribes into the modern era as they simultaneously whittled away their tribal rights. The meeting house reared proudly over the town of wooden cabins and stores on mud streets.

Heck eased the wagon, which they had found behind the trading store at Cut-Throat Crossroads, in before the building. A group of Indians had gathered to admire the Appaloosa and quarter horse, then gawp at the contents of the wagon. 'You better keep your eye on 'em,' he advised Zeke.

He climbed the steps and went through the decorative doorway. 'No dancing' a notice warned in English and Choctaw.

'I weren't planning to,' the marshal muttered, as a Choctaw woman showed him into the office of Chief Allen Wright, who was in formal dress, frock coat, striped trousers, white linen and loose bow tie. Even his greying hair was cut short, white man-style, and parted on one side.

'Howdy, chief,' Heck said, shaking hands. 'Some place you got here.'

'Yes, how you like my desk?' The chief beamed, proudly, and indicated the other furnishings, carpets, clock, and cuspidor. 'These alone cost two thousand dollar. What your business, Marshal?'

'I got a bunch of corpses outside I'd like you to take a look at. We had a bit of trouble out at

Cut-throat Crossroads.'

The five corpses were laid out in the back of the wagon, their putrefying, fly-buzzing flesh ripening redolently in the hot sun.

'Big Gus, the storekeeper,' Allen Wright said, identifying him. 'It is a fitting fate. He cheated my people. I did not know he used guns.'

'You sure he meant to back-shoot me with that twelve gauge, Zeke?'

'Sure as sure. It was you or him. I could see it on his face. I ain't proud of shootin' Jim Lee in the back. But, agin, I had to or you would have gone down, Marshal.'

'Guess I owe you,' Thomas said.

'They were the first men I ever killed,' Zeke muttered, the shock of the slayings that had all seemed to happen in gun-crashing seconds still within him.

'How about these two?' Heck pointed at the Mexican and the unknown man.

'No, I have never seen them before.' The chief shrugged. 'Gus kept bad company. This is where it leads to.'

'We're taking these two.' Heck pointed to the Lees. 'Can you bury t'others, Mr Wright?' He put a pouch of silver in the chief's hands. 'This is what small change we found on 'em. Should cover it. And there's a store looking for a new owner out at the crossing. One of your people might like to go into business.'

'No, that place is haunted. Too many deaths.'

'Well, the blankets and stuff ain't haunted. It's there for the taking.'

'What about her?' the chief asked, and nodded at the Indian woman, who squatted amid the corpses, her expression wooden.

'She attacked my deputy.' Heck touched Zeke's bloodily bandaged arm. 'A case of misplaced loyalty, no doubt. We ain't pressing charges.'

'What can we do with her? She is disgraced. Her family will not have her back.'

The lawmen tumbled the unwanted corpses out of the wagon and told the woman to clear off. 'Maybe you can give her a job cleanin' up an' cookin' in your nice new meeting house?'

'Do these two come under your jurisdiction, Marshal?' Wright asked, peering at the Lees. 'What is their crime?'

'They killed four of my men. That's jurisdiction enough for me.' Heck climbed to the front of the wagon and gathered the reins. 'We've been on their trail for nigh on two months.'

'They belong to you,' the chief said. 'Can I offer you my hospitality, Marshal?'

'Thanks, but no. Gotta be on our way,' Heck said. 'By the way, there was another man, Ned Christie. If you see anythang of him you tell him we'll be back one day. He won't get away.'

'Ah, yes, a Cherokee. He used to be a tribal councillor but went to the bad.'

'Waal, if you people's own leaders have started peddling rum we sure got a battle on our hands,' Heck sang out, putting the wagon in motion. 'So long, Chief.'

Zeke's heart quickened as they drove along the Ouachita trail, vast swathes of oak and pine mantling the hillsides. 'Where's all the cattle gawn?' he asked, as they approached the ranch house. 'Pull in by the dogwood a sec, Heck. I wanna cut one of them snowy blossoms fer that purty Indian gal.'

'Don't tell me you're entranced with her, too?' the marshal muttered, but did as suggested.

Ice came from a barn door, a rifle in her hands pointed their way as they drove in, but she put it up and smiled when she recognized them. 'What brings you here?' she asked.

Heck brandished a leather bag of gold and silver coins. 'Here's all that remained of the cash they stole from your husband. Nine hundred dollars.' He tossed it to her. 'It's yours.'

'Mine?' Ice, in her white buckskin dress, stared at the pouch, nonplussed.

'Sure. You're entitled to it. I hoped your brother-in-law, Alva, might be here,' the marshal replied. 'I got business with him.'

'No, he came with his men and herded the cattle away. They took them north to the Kansas markets. Alva went back to Gainesville. He promised to pay me my share.' A weatherbeaten cowboy had followed her from the barn, a rifle in his hands, too. 'He left Hank here for my protection.'

'Huh.' Zeke jumped down, eyed the man. 'He did, did he?' He grinned as he presented Ice with the bouquet. 'See who we caught.' He showed her the two corpses. 'Is that them?'

She stared at the two dead men for moments. 'Yes, that is them. How could I ever forget?'

'Aincha pleased?' Zeke was troubled because the girl seemed troubled.

'I am only pleased,' she said, meeting his blue eyes, 'that it is not you who is dead.'

101

'You are?' He grinned even wider. 'Aw, you ain't no need to worry about me. I can look after myself.'

Over supper in the ranch house their eyes kept locking and Zeke was feeling pretty elated one way or the other. When Ice said she had to go outside to lock up the hen house and stables Zeke stepped out, too, and waited on the porch for her return. The sky had darkened, the stars popping out, silhouetting the line of forested hills. 'Must git purty lonesome here,' he said, when she returned.

'Hank is company.'

'Oh, yuh? He ain't been cosyin' up to you, has he?'

'Cosying up?' Ice smiled with surprise. 'Why? Is that what you would like to do?'

Zeke fumbled with his hat, wanting to grab the girl and kiss her, but shy to. 'No, I guess I ain't got no right. I already got a gal. I gotta be honest with you, I'm promised to Pearl Starr. I asked her to marry me.'

Ice's expression became sombre, almost icy. 'I should tell you, Zeke, my father is a chief of his tribe. So that I should be safe in all the trouble after the war he sent me to the school run by nuns at Tishomingo. They taught me to speak and write English, to worship the one God and his son, Jesus, and that it is wrong, as our people do, to have several wives. You had better go to Pearl.'

'Aw, I—'

At that point Hank came from the wooden house and mumbled, 'Goodnight all, I'm gonna turn in early.' He ambled, bowlegged, his chaps flapping, over to the bunkhouse.

'No.' Ice smiled. 'You see, he is not cosying up to me.'

'Guess we'd better turn in, too,' the marshal said, as he, too, came from the house. 'Wanna be up 'fore dawn, make an early start for Gainesville. You comin', Zeke?'

As he turned to follow, Ice caught hold of his arm. 'Does it not bother you, Zeke, what those men did to me?'

'They're dead, you're alive,' Zeke said. 'That's what matters to me.'

The Chickasaw girl stared at him, tears welling in her dark eyes. 'Thank you. Take care, Zeke.'

'You planning to claim that reward Mr Roff was offering?' Zeke asked, as they trundled away on the wagon in the half light of dawn. 'That ain't like

103

you. Thought you allus played by the book, Marshal.'

'Maybe I'm tired of playing by the book, of being a poor man, like Marshal Guy was. If there's a reward us two have earned it. Maybe the judge won't like it, but the judge ain't gonna be gettin' it.'

'Gee!' Zeke stroked his jaw. 'We'll be rich. What you gonna do with your share, Marshal?'

'I intend to give five hundred dollars to Big Jim's widow.'

'Yeah,' Zeke promised. 'I'll do that, too.'

'That won't leave us exactly rich, but it's better than a dollar apiece. That's if we get it. C'mon, giddap.' Heck flicked the reins at the cart horse as their own two trotted along behind. 'We got a hundred miles to go to the ferry over the Red. Then another coupla hundred through Paris, Texas, and on to Gainesville.'

'Yes suh,' Zeke repeated. 'That's what we'll do.'

'I'll tell ya what, boys,' Alva Roff yelled, as he surveyed the Lees' putrescent corpses. 'You not only get my two and a half thousand bucks' reward, I'm gonna add the thousand five hundred gov'ment of Texas reward on these two. That makes two thou' each.'

He led them into his ranch house study and wrote two separate cheques to be drawn on Wells Fargo bank at Fort Smith. He presented them to the lawmen. 'That fair?'

'Half each is fair,' Heck said, glancing at his young deputy. 'We both risked our lives.'

'I want to thank you. My brothers have been avenged,' the rangy Texan replied, offering his hand to shake. 'Now I'd better take them two buzzards into town, git their photograph picture, identify 'em to the town sheriff and apply for the gov'ment reward. That'll take time, but it'll come through. Maybe I'd better not mention your part in this in case Judge Parker hears about it. Hear tell the Hanging Judge is quite a stickler.'

'Yeah.' Heck nodded, tucking his cheque into his pocket. 'Maybe you better not. Don't wanna rustle the old rooster's feathers.'

Back outside they unhitched their horses and swung aboard. 'We'll leave you the wagon, Alva,' Heck called. 'Oh, by the way, there's a few bottles of rum in a tarpaulin bag we confiscated. It's yours.'

'Don't you drink?' the rancher asked.

'Only a glass of wine now and again.' Heck gave

his rare smile as he nudged the quarter horse away.
'And I don't wanna start this young galoot drinkin''
that fiery stuff. It's the sure road to ruination.'

TWELVE

German-born George Maledon carefully sorted through the collection of nooses hanging on the walls of his workroom amid pictures of now-dead felons and his Press cuttings. He was a very meticulous fellow and used only the best rope money could buy, Kentucky hemp, shipped all the way to Fort Smith by riverboat from St Louis.

'These are three nice uns,' he muttered, for he was preparing for a triple hanging. Rarely a week went by without one. 'These'll give 'em a neat send-off.'

The bushy-bearded George did not like to see his clients kicking and struggling for minutes at a time as in some messy hangings and lynchings. No, he strove to ensure a good, clean descent into the gates of Hell.

After oiling the ropes he took them outside and climbed the twelve steps to his beloved gibbet. He attached each one to a 200lb sandbag, jerked the trigger arm and watched them drop in unison. 'Perfect!' he hissed.

There was a clattering of horse's hoofs and he saw Judge Parker riding his big, eighteen-hand bay stallion around the building from the stables. 'Mornin', ya Honour. You're out early.'

Indeed, the eastern sky was bright melon-coloured, the sun yet to appear, and a big silver half-moon still clearly showed. 'You, too, George, forever fussing over your gallows.'

'I need to stretch these ropes. That'll thin 'em down to a sturdy inch circumference. It seems a shame we've never dropped a dozen at a time. That's what I designed the twenty foot long trapdoor fer and that great crossbeam would easily take their weight. It's finest oak.'

'Yes, well, I think we'd better stick to the occasional half-dozen in view of some criticism from Washington, ill-informed as it might be.'

'Aw, don't you take no notice of them, sir. We're cleaning the world of the refuse of humanity. I've never known one of them demons who stepped up here who didn't deserve to die.'

'Quite.' A giant of a man, Isaac Parker had little difficulty controlling the restless stallion. 'Be sure to give the trap hinges a drop of oil.'

'I will, ya Honour,' Maledon replied with relish. 'Where you go each marnin' on that fine brute?'

'Oh, along the river and up through the woods.' The judge waved his riding crop vaguely. 'Satan needs to exercise and so do I. If I sat in court each and every day without some strenuous exercise beforehand my mind would never be sharp.'

'It worries me, sir,' Maledon cautioned. 'Surely you didn't ought to ride out so far without a bodyguard. There's some bad uns about.'

'If anybody wishes to assassinate me I'm sure they could do so as easily in Fort Smith.' The judge looked as impatient as the horse to be away. 'I'll be back in hour or so, Mr Maledon. Keep up the good work.'

'Oh, I will, sir. You can rely on me.' Maledon watched the judge go charging away, once clear of the houses giving the horse its head to gallop along the bank of the wide Arkansas. 'A man needs his exercise, that's fer sure.'

Fort Smith's jurisdiction was larger than any other

court in history, its wild terrain reaching all the way from Arkansas to the Colorado border, and Judge Parker's word was law. Such were the distances to be travelled, and the dangers braved by his marshals and deputies, he was lenient of the fact that they might be out on the trail for months at a time. If they did not bring in their man alive, however, they forfeited expenses.

'Waal, that won't worry us,' Zeke mused, as he trotted along on the Appaloosa beside Marshal Thomas. He patted the cheque in his shirt pocket. 'Never dreamed I was gonna be so wealthy.'

'If you've got any sense you'll stick that in the bank, build up a nest egg,' the marshal replied. 'You could easy get injured or crippled in this game. You won't git no retirement pension, mark my words.'

'Aw, I'll be OK,' Zeke sang out, breezily. 'I was born under a lucky star. I'm gonna send five hundred dollars to my folks and five hundred to Widow Guy. That'll leave me a thousand.'

'Just don't go wasting it on whiskey and wimmin, that's all I'm saying. You could do with some new duds. We both could. The judge likes his men to look smart.'

They had made good time riding hundreds of

miles back from the Choctaw country, reaching the Arkansas at the spot where work was starting on the new bridge.

'The railroads are starting to edge into the territory. That'll sound the death-knell for shallow-draught paddlers on the Arkansas,' Heck observed. 'At one time there'd be fifteen or so tied up at Fort Gibson. Times sure are changin'. There's talk of throwing the whole of Indian Territory open to settlement.'

Impatient to get back to Fort Smith for hot baths, clean clothes and meals eaten with their legs under a table, rather than squatted in all weathers over smoky camp-fires, on this last morning they had set off before dawn.

The sun's rays were edging over the horizon as, taking a short cut, they rode through a forest glade towards the fort. Suddenly Heck spotted a cabin laid back in the pines, blue woodsmoke spiralling from its chimney.

'Hello,' he said, reining in. 'This place used to be derelict. I wonder who's taken up residence here?'

Marshal Thomas was a naturally suspicious man. 'Let's take a look,' he said, stepping down, loosening his sidearm in its holster. 'You never

111

know who might be hidin' out in the woods.'

Both lawmen hitched their mounts to a tree bough, and stepped carefully through the scrub towards the back of the cabin. 'There's a big hoss tied up out front,' Zeke remarked. 'Looks all steamed up.'

'Yeah, and a pony and fancy rig in here,' Heck replied, peering into a stable door. 'Funny.'

The dawn light had yet to penetrate the close-packed pines and it was still very gloomy. A lantern was lit in a back room, its window covered by curtains. There was the sound of voices and a creaking movement from inside. Heck got up close and put his eye to a crack in the curtains. 'Hot ziggity!' he exclaimed, and turned his head away, his expression shocked. 'I'd never have believed it.'

'What?' Zeke hissed.

'No.' The marshal put up an arm. 'It ain't for your eyes.'

'Come on.' Zeke pressed him aside and peeked in, himself. 'My God!'

It was true. He would never have believed it, either. He could not unglue his eye from the crack in the curtain. A small brass bed creaking rythmically as it thumped the wall. Pearl Starr, naked but for black silk stockings and her saucy hat was knelt upon it, a large man, his trousers around his knees, juddered at her faster than a fiddler's elbow. Suddenly he moved position to reveal a shock of thick black hair, an aquiline nose, and a jutting goatee beard. 'It's the judge!' Zeke hissed.

'Come on.' Marshal Thomas jerked him away. 'We ain't Peeping Toms.'

'But—' Zeke protested, looking similarly shocked. 'That's my gal. That's the gal I love. What's that dirty bastard doin'?'

'What do you think he's doin'?' Thomas pulled him further away. 'Does she look like she's objecting? Pah!' He shook the youth by his neckerchief. 'Ye've seen for yourself. She's a cheap li'l chiseller. Like her mother, a Jezebel of the deepest dye. One of the scarlet sisterhood. It's just as well ye've seen with your own eyes. Still plannin' on marrying her, are ye?'

'OK.' Zeke stopped protesting, as if sobering up. 'I've seen what I've seen.'

'Right, we'll give 'em ten minutes then we'll go in.'

'What? Are you crazy?'

'Maybe I am. Maybe we're risking our jobs. But

113

I believe the judge should be aware that we know what a damn hypocrite he is.'

'I guess,' Zeke mused, quietly, 'he's got his needs, like any man, to judge from that frosty-faced wife of his. Jeez! You see the way they were doin' it? I never knew you could do it like that.'

This elicited a faint smile from the marshal. 'There's a lot you don't know, son.'

'What you gonna do?'

'Watch.' The marshal led the way around to the front. 'Their time is up.'

He hammered on the door.' Judge!' he boomed. 'Open up.'

Heck listened and gave another grim smile, lowering his voice. 'They're whispering and scrabbling around in there like rats in a hole knowing they're trapped.'

Zeke grinned and joined in, banging on the door and yelling, 'We know you're in there, Judge. We got urgent business.'

'Leave this to me,' Heck said, and shouted again. 'This is Marshal Thomas. I wanna talk to you, Judge Parker.'

He listened again. Eventually, the door was unbolted and Parker peered out through a three-inch crack. 'Just go away, Mr Thomas,' he ordered.

'I'll speak to you back at Fort Smith.'

Zeke gave the marshal a hefty push in the back and the door was thrown open. Yielding to the unexpected, the judge stepped back into the small kitchen-living room and the lawmen followed him. 'What is the meaning of this?' Parker roared.

He was a hefty, broad-chested man, standing in a collarless shirt, suspenders over his shoulders now holding up his striped pants. He tried to scrape his hair from his eyes. 'You'd better have a good explanation.'

'Maybe you ought to have that, Judge,' Heck said. 'We were passing and I seen Satan. Just wondered what you were doing in this back of beyond. Thought maybe you needed some help.'

'No, I don't need any help. If you must know I come here to have some quiet, get on with some work. Now will you kindly leave?'

'Some sorta work,' Zeke yelped, dodging past his bulky form and into the back bedroom. 'Waal, lookee who's here!'

Pearl had pulled on a skimpy lace negligée with a feather collar, which didn't do much to disguise her naked, hour-glass form. She jogged one stockinged leg over the other and gave a mischievous smirk. 'Well, if it ain't the virgin cowboy! You gotta nerve comin' in here.'

'You allus wear your hat in bed?'

'All right. This will ruin me if it gets out.' The judge had come in and was pulling on his frock coat. 'Is that what you want, gentlemen?'

'No, we don't want that,' Heck muttered.

'Well, why not jine us?' Pearl piped up. 'How about a foursome? I don't mind. Like they say, if you got the money, honey, I got the time.'

'How much does he pay you, Pearl?' Zeke demanded, indignant as an outraged husband. 'How long has this been going on?'

'Aw, Belle was servicing him for a while 'til she got a bit scrawny for this old buzzard's taste. So she passed me on to him. Ain't that so, Isaac? Ain't you ever wondered, Marshal, why your evidence aginst Ma allus gits thrown out?'

'I must say it's passed through my mind. Same as with her lover boy, Blue Duck. Why *didn't* you have him hanged, Your Honour?'

Parker sat back on the bed beside Pearl, looking dazed. 'You've got me over a barrel. It's the truth. What can I say? How much do you two want to forget this?'

'We don't want your cash, Judge.' Heck gave him a look of distaste. 'True, if the journals get hold of this you're a dead duck. And I guess Mrs Parker might take a dim view, too.'

The marshal paused for effect, stroking his jaw, letting his words sink in and then drawled, 'But there's no reason why anyone other than us should hear of this. Pearl here knows it would be wise not to tittle-tattle for her own health – if you get my meaning, girl – and, no doubt, for her own financial advantage. I'll forget what I've seen today, so will Zeke, if he's any sense.'

'Will I?' Zeke said. 'Yes, I s'pose. I guess I gotta forgive you, Pearl.'

'All we're asking, Judge, is that if we ever catch Belle Starr up to her dirty tricks again and we bring her before you she gets due punishment. It'll be up to her then whether she says anything about you, or not.'

The judge sat and considered this ultimatum, breathing hard, as if he knew his life had been saved. 'Thank you, Mr Thomas,' he said, tying a scarf around his neck. 'I will bear what you say in mind.'

'You better had, sir,' Heck warned him. 'I'd hate for any of this to get out.'

'Hey,' Pearl cooed. 'Don't I get a say in it?'

'No you don't,' the marshal snapped. 'And you

117

can tell that disreputable mother of yourn she better watch her step from now on.'

'Sorry we interrupted your morning ride, sir.' Zeke grinned and slapped Parker on his shoulder. 'Guess we'd better be on our way.'

'Yes,' Parker muttered, like a man in a trance. 'I've got to be in court at eight.'

THIRTEEN

When he had soaked in a hot tub, been shaved, had his hair trimmed, and dressed in a new off-the-peg brown tweed suit, with a soft blue shirt and loose bow that night, Zeke made his way along the crowded sidewalk of Fort Smith. He was mildly surprised to find Pearl in the Horse's Leg saloon sitting insouciantly on the bench reserved for the dancing girls as if she hadn't a care in the world.

'Howdy,' he said. 'Fancy a spin?'

He had hung his hat and gunbelt on a peg, bought a handful of tickets, and pushed through the throng of dancers to lean on the pole that corralled the girls off from any frisky men.

Pearl's cheek dimpled, mischievously, and she glanced at her saucy friends. 'Just look at you,' she said. 'All duded up. More like a gambling man than a marshal.'

'Yeah, I even gave my boots and spurs a shine.' He grinned at her. 'I drew two months' back pay, eighty dollars, so blew it on these fancy duds.'

'Whoo! Listen to him! A real big spender.' She squeezed past her pals. 'In that case I guess I better oblige.'

Zeke's toe was tapping to the melodies pumped out from the podium by a banjo-plucking, fiddle-screeching, piano-jangling trio, and he caught her by the waist and whisked her away into the giddy whirl.

'So, you ain't angry with me?' Pearl cried, as she hung onto him. 'You ain't gonna cause any trouble?'

'I must admit it sure was a shock,' he replied, 'to see you and you know who. I thought you and me were engaged.'

'What?' she shrieked above the din. 'You go off for two months without a word and expect me to live like a nun? You mighta been gunned down for all I knew.'

'Yuh, well, I weren't. We put paid to them Lees.'

'You did? Well, whadda ya know?'

She hugged her pert breasts harder into him.

'So you forgive me?'

Zeke met her merry, teasing eyes. 'Yep, I guess.'

It was too noisy and the dancing too fast and furious to say much more. But after three more whirls he yelled, 'Wow! I'm gonna grab me a beer.'

Pearl held onto his hand as he headed for the bar. 'I'll have a wine and soda.'

'Are you allowed to?' Zeke asked.

'Sure.' Her eyes twinkled. 'I can do what I darn well like. That's the best of working here. It ain't like being one of them poor cows stuck in The Row, mauled from morning to night by every drunken oaf with two dollars to spare. Here I get plenty of free time and I can pick and choose which gentlemen I see.'

Zeke took a gulp of his steam beer and gazed at her. 'I still want to take you away from this life. We could go to California.'

'What?' she squealed. 'What on? Buttons? How much you say a deputy makes? Forty-a-month? Are you joking?'

They had found a quieter spot behind a pillar. 'To tell the truth, Pearl, I'm tired of being a deputy marshal. You're right. There's no cash, no future in it. Except—'

'Except what?'

121

He glanced around to make sure they weren't overheard. 'Howja like to make ten thousand dollars?'

'Ten thou'?' She gave an impish grin. 'Tell me another, buster. What you been drinkin' 'fore that beer?'

'This is the truth. I've been offered a secret mission. They want me to guard a Wells Fargo consignment going from here to their new bank in Fort Gibson. It'll be in a strongbox on a stagecoach of their'n. I'm s'posed to act as shotgun.'

Pearl licked her lips, unsure whether to believe him. 'Ten thousand?'

'No.' He lowered his voice. 'There'll be twenty thousand in gold and silver and paper money in that box. I've been to see them today to arrange the details.'

Pearl's eyes nearly popped out of her head. 'Twenty thousand?'

'Yes. I thought your mother, Belle, Sam Starr and their men could hold up the coach. I hand over the cash. We share it. Ten thousand for them, ten thousand for us.'

Pearl studied the handsome young deputy for moments, his honest blue eyes anxiously meeting hers. It would be like taking candy from a baby.

'Are you serious, Zeke?'

'Yes. But there's one catch. The stage is due to move out the day after tomorrow. You wouldn't have time to get in touch with Belle. Pity, ain't it?'

Pearl patted his hand. 'You just wait here a minute, sweetheart.'

He sipped his beer and watched her weave through the crowd, speak to the proprietor, and go upstairs to the rooms above. A short while later she re-emerged on the landing and beckoned him. Trying to look inconspicuous Zeke ambled across and up the stairs to her.

'Come on,' Pearl said. 'It's all settled.'

She opened a door and pushed him inside. Belle Starr and her husband, Sam, were sitting either side of a small table. 'Meet the folks,' Pearl purred.

'We've met before,' Belle said. 'Hiya, handsome.'

'Hi.' Zeke sat on a bed with Pearl beside him. 'So you've heard my proposition?'

'We sure have, cowboy.' Belle was rigged out in her long, English-style riding dress so she could go side-saddle on her favourite horse, Venus. A velvet jacket, the ostrich-feathered hat, inlaid boots, and a big six-shooter holstered on her belt, completed the outfit. 'It sounds interesting. But how do we know you're on the level?'

'He damn well better be,' Sam growled, 'or I pity him.'

'I'm on the level,' Zeke said, 'because I want to marry your daughter. And for that, to make a new life, we need cash. Ten thousand for me and Pearl and ten thousand for you. No shooting, no trouble. Couldn't be easier.'

'How come they've chose you for this job?' Belle's dark, beady eyes flickered distrust but also greed. 'That's what I don't understand.'

'I guess because I'm relatively unknown so I won't draw attention to the consignment.' He gave a slight smile. 'Or perhaps your friend the judge had something to do with it.'

'What you think, Sam?' Belle asked, after she had fired some more questions at Zeke. 'Shall we go for it?'

The Cherokee flicked his long black hair out of his eyes, took out his revolver, clicked the cylinder around, and cocked it, while he held it on Zeke. 'Why not? If it's a trick he'll be the first to die.'

'It ain't no trick,' Zeke assured them, for it went through his mind that these two were behind innumerable killings, torture, extortion, robbery, rustling and horse thieving for which they'd never been brought to account. 'You think I'm stupid, or what?'

'I won't answer that.' Belle grinned and got to her feet, flicking a riding quirt hanging from her wrist at him. 'So, you and my li'l gal are gonna seek pastures new in California, huh! Guess I'll have to give you my blessing.'

'Gee, thanks, Ma.' Pearl sprang up and gave her a hug and kiss and, as she moved back a slight wink. 'Just think, Wednesday we'll all be rich.'

'Yes,' Zeke said, enthusiastically. 'I've had a bellyful of being a deputy marshal and putting my life on the line for peanuts. I thought maybe the best place to strike would be Weber Falls. It's a lonesome stretch of trail. We should be there at noon.'

'You throw down the box and go on your way?' Belle mused. 'We meet you back at Younger's Bend? It couldn't be simpler, could it? What think you, Sam?'

The Cherokee stared at the youngster, aggressively. Then shrugged. 'Wednesday at noon it is.'

Three children were playing a macabre game on

the steps of the gallows as Marshal Thomas walked into the stockade. The hangman's daughter, Annie, had a noose in her hands, putting it over the head of one of the judge's sons as the other looked on and pretended to applaud.

'What on earth are you doing?' Heck shouted, as Annie pushed the boy and he jumped to the ground. 'That's no game to play. Where did you get that noose?'

'From Papa's workroom.' At twelve Annie was a remarkably beautiful girl, her blonde hair hanging down to the small of her back, her eyes vividly green in their upturned white slots. 'He doesn't mind.'

'He don't mind if he don't know. I bet that's more the case. He'd be furious and your ma would be horrified. You know she won't have anything like that in the house.'

'It's only a game.' Annie, in a blue gingham dress and white stockings, pouted her lips, sulkily. The marshal couldn't help but notice that she was budding out, becoming more female in form. It occurred to him that George would have his hands full in a couple of years keeping boys from buzzing about her. Annie was too pretty for her own good. 'I'm bored,' she said, as if reading his thoughts.

'I'm not allowed to leave the stockade. I have to play with these two. I didn't mean any harm.'

'Maybe not,' the marshal replied. 'But there might be an accident. You take that rope back and put it back where you found it and promise never to take it again, Then I won't have to say anything to your father, nor,' he added, turning to the boys, 'to the judge, either.'

They looked so crestfallen he put his hand in his pocket and brought out some liquorice and a bag of bull's eyes. 'Look what I brought you. I nearly forgot. Now no more playing on these gallows. You hear?'

'Yes, sir,' the boys chorused, but when Marshal Thomas turned his back to go into the big courthouse building Annie stuck out her tongue and remarked, defiantly, 'He's no right to talk to me like that.'

Girls not much older than Annie were often married in these frontier parts. Heck Thomas had often wished that he could have had children, but it occurred to him that keeping youngsters on the right path was a more than difficult job.

The incident had reminded him of Alice, a young woman not dissimilar in looks to Annie Maledon.

It struck at him again, like a bolt from the blue, as it always did, the memory of that day years ago. They had planned to marry. But it was not to be. One moment Heck was taking his lady love for a quiet Sunday drive in his buggy. The next they were attacked by three assassins. Heck returned fire. When he had killed all three he turned and found that Alice was dying, too, a bullet in her chest. That was the worst day of the marshal's life. It had been a revenge attack by criminals he had given evidence against and had seen jailed many months before. After that Heck seriously considered giving up law enforcement.

But he had stayed in the job and maybe that accounted for the relentless manner in which he pursued wrongdoers. Young Zeke had remarked that Judge Parker, 'had his needs'. Well, so had every red-blooded man. It was a matter of learning to control such desires. Heck Thomas himself had no taste for common prostitutes. Often he had wished that he could meet a decent young woman. But it would not be fair to her to expose her to the danger that he faced on a regular basis. No, he could not risk it. He had to remain alone. Zeke seemed to think he had been a tad hard on Parker. But a man in such a position should not have consorted with the most notorious female criminal in the territory. Such madness invited corruption and blackmail.

Heck, sitting alone with a coffee in the canteen, was aroused from such melancholy thoughts by the noisy arrival of Frank Dalton and his boisterous younger brothers, Grat, Bob and Emmett, who had recently been enrolled as deputies.

Grat gave a whoop, wielding a carbine. 'We're going out to kill a few whiskey hawkers,' he yelled.

'If you consult our book of rules,' Heck cautioned, 'you'll see that we're s'posed to bring 'em in alive, if at all possible.'

Emmett grinned. 'What's the fun in that?'

Frank Dalton, who had served honourably for three years as a deputy marshal, explained. 'We heard there's hawkers operating openly out of Muskogee. The judge has told us to go get 'em.'

'You'd better tell those boys to calm down. I get a distinct feeling your brothers are too wild for this job,' Heck remarked. 'That they view a deputy's badge as a licence to kill.'

'Don't worry, Marshal,' Frank called out, as they clattered off to get their horses. 'I'll make sure they obey the rules.'

FOURTEEN

Zeke held on tight with one hand to his precarious seat on the box of the Wells Fargo coach as it went creaking and swaying, rocking and bouncing down the rutted trail into the gulch. In his other hand he gripped his Winchester carbine. Too Morrow, the driver, strained back on the reins, shouting to the four horses to slow down. It was high noon, and they were fast approaching Weber Falls.

When they reached the flat among willows alongside the river-bank they suddenly saw three masked men on mustangs, revolvers raised in their hands, move out of the trees in front of them, shouting, threateningly.

'Whoa thar,' Too screeched hoarsely, bringing the coach to a halt.

'Throw that strongbox down,' the leading horseman barked out, his Colt aimed at Zeke. 'But, first, lay aside that Winchester, pal. Don't try no tricks.'

Now they were stopped, Zeke could clearly hear the roar of the falls not far off. He glanced around and saw two more masked horsemen on the ridge about ninety feet above them, carbines at the ready, watching on. He carefully laid his Winchester back on the roof of the coach, leaned down and hauled the strongbox out from beneath his seat. He tipped it over to land in the sun-firmed mud. 'I ain't arguing,' he said, giving the lead robber a wink.

The gunman jumped down from his horse, fired a shot into the lock and opened the box. He picked up a handful of washers and cursed. 'Lousy washers!' he yelled, and swung his Colt round on to Zeke.

Before he could fire, Marshal Thomas poked his .45 through the buckskin curtain of the coach window and pumped two shots into him.

George Maledon jumped from the other side of the coach, a revolver in each hand. Both barrels spat lead and another of the masked men rolled from his saddle.

Zeke reached for his Winchester as a bullet smashed into the woodwork where he had just been sitting. 'Up there,' he yelled, pointing to the two horsemen on the ridge. They were letting loose a volley of lead.

'Hell take 'em,' Too Morrow croaked, as he scrambled down to safety on the far side of the coach.

Both Marshal Thomas and Maledon returned fire, sending a tattoo of bullets whistling towards the bushwhackers up above. Suddenly it was as if a big rock had hit Zeke in the chest. He tumbled from the top of the coach to lay in the mud gasping for breath. Blood was pumping from his shirt. 'Aw, Jeez,' he groaned, as the ground beneath him seemed to spin. 'I'm hit!' were the last words he spoke as a blanket of blackness enclosed him. . . .

'Those are the ones we want.' Heck sent a last bullet flying at the two road agents on the ridge. But they had seen enough, hauling their mustangs around and heading away.

The third man in front of the coach decided this might be a good idea, too, circling his mount around, making towards the falls. He did not get

far. The hangman raised one of his long-barrelled
.45s, his arm outstretched, and took careful aim.
The gunman threw up his hands and was pitched
to the ground to go bouncing along, one boot
caught in the stirrup. 'That's another hanging fee
I've lost.' Maledon growled.

Heck Thomas lost no time. He caught one of
the dead men's horses, jumped into the saddle,
and set after the runaways. Maledon coaxed the
other horse to him, struggled on to it, and
pounded away after the marshal.

It was not unusual for Belle Starr to put on
men's garb if, occasionally, she rode out with her
gang. It began when she was seventeen and held
up a coach in Texas with Cole Younger. Most
memorable was some years before when she and
Sam had tortured an old Creek Indian and his
squaw until they revealed a cache of twenty
thousand in gold coin.

Nor, this time, had she been unable to resist
disguising herself again at the prospect of another
$20,000 falling into their hands. But this time her
greed had been her undoing. 'The bastard tricked
us,' she cried, as she and Sam went galloping away
from Weber Falls.

'He paid the price,' Sam Starr shouted. 'Like I

warned him he would.'

It was rough country, but they knew the terrain and settled their mounts into a steady lope, unworried by the possibility of any pursuit.

They followed the curve of the river and, after covering ten miles in good time, they reached a quiet spot amid some high rocks where they had left their spare horses fresh for another fast ride back into the Nations.

Belle divested herself of her hat, her topcoat, her boots, and began kicking off her pair of men's baggy pants. She pulled a long skirt on over her stockings, and the boots back on her feet. Then she found her ostrich-feathered hat, pulling it down, military-style, over her brow.

'Come on, Venus.' She fondled the patiently waiting big grey and swung on to her back. 'We're going home.'

The long-haired Indian, Sam Starr, was about to put spurs to his fresh mount to lead the way when a voice rang out. 'You ain't going nowhere 'cept Fort Worth dungeon.'

Heck Thomas appeared, standing on top of one of the rocks, his revolver cocked and ready for shooting, like some stern Minister of Justice.

'I wouldn't try anythang,' the hangman yelled,

trotting his mustang into the clearing behind them.

Belle's hand went automatically to the long revolver holstered at her waist. But Sam Starr was more circumspect, tossing his hair from his eyes and smiling. 'What you talking about, Marshal?'

'Yes.' Belle, too, put on air of innocence. 'Can't we go out for a ride without being pestered by you? Why are you always harassing us?'

'Ar, shut up,' Heck rejoined. 'Just drop your gunbelts. You're coming with us to Fort Smith.'

'Why?' Belle protested. 'On what trumped-up charge?'

'Attempted mail robbery and murder,' Maledon growled, his white beard waggling, angrily. 'I cain't wait to git my ropes around your necks. That's why I volunteered for this expedition.'

Heck picked up the discarded clothing and took a look at the brands on the sweated-up mustangs. 'Looks like there'll be another charge of horse stealing,' he drawled. 'Come on, get moving you two. You know the way back to the coach. We need to get there double quick.'

FIFTEEN

At first he was shivering with cold, as if he had fallen through lake ice and could not reach the surface. And then he was screaming with pain as the army surgeon's knife cut into him and he believed himself burning in the flames of hell, thrashing about, twisting and turning. When he finally awoke into the calm of the night in a hospital ward Zeke Jones knew only the throbbing numbness of his stitched up wound. He lay wondering where he could be. Panic hit him as he realized there was no feeling in his left arm. It lay inert, unresponding to his mental effort to operate it.

'So you've decided to come back to us, have you?' the orderly said, when he heard his groan of

136

horror. 'I thought you were headed for the Vale of Shadows.'

It was only through coach driver Too Morrow's quick thinking that Zeke was alive at all. He had plugged his gaping wound so, although he lost a lot of blood, it was not fatal. When the marshal and the hangman had returned they had carefully transported him to Fort Gibson where he was attended to by the surgeon in the infirmary. He had dug out the bullet, which had missed any vital organs, but was lodged awkwardly under a bone.

'You been in some deep fever for a week or so. It was touch and go,' the orderly told him. 'The sawbones said you might end up not being able to use that arm. Seems like the nerves were damaged.'

'You mean I'm gonna be a cripple the rest of my life?'

'Think yourself lucky you're alive, boy. Most men who get deep gunshot wounds in the chest gen'rally end up dead from blood pizening.'

But it took some getting used to: a shocking prospect. Even when he got back on his feet and began getting exercise his left arm hung inert, slightly crooked at the elbow, the palm of his hand upraised, fingers open. Not a twitch. Not the slightest feeling. He would be a one-armed man from here in.

When he eventually caught the tri-weekly stage back to Fort Smith Zeke had yet another shock. Marshal Thomas tried to break it to him as gently as possible, but he was being honourably discharged from the service. 'I don't make the rules, Zeke,' he said, 'but the fact is that if you're unfit and you ain't got two hands to hold a carbine then we can't keep you on.'

All the marshal could give him was two weeks back-pay covering his stay in the infirmary and a week's severance pay. 'I guess you're lucky you hung on to some of that reward money. That should see you through until you've sorted yourself out.'

'Lucky? You can say that again!'

'Ain't no use being bitter, Zeke. You were aware of the risks when you joined the service. We're all walking that tightrope.'

'You figure Sam Starr was the one who shot me?'

'Either him or Belle. They're both killers. I'm gonna press hard for life sentences.'

'Some hope. I bet they both walk off scot free.'

'Are you satisfied, Marshal?' Judge Parker asked

after he had sentenced Belle and Sam Starr both to a year's imprisonment for horse thieving.

'It's a start,' the marshal muttered, grimly, as they were removed from the dock in shackles to be sent down-river to the penitentiary.

The Starrs had come up with an alibi, a carter who, through fear or bribery, swore that he had passed them on the trail fifteen miles from Weber Falls at exactly noon on the day in question. The charges of attempted murder and attempted robbery were thrown out for lack of identifying evidence.

Zeke had holed up in a boarding-house at Fort Smith. He was taking a rest one afternoon after the hearing for he was still not recovered from the shock to his system and loss of blood. There was a tap on the door and Pearl Starr sashayed into his room in a candy-striped hat to match her candy-striped satin dress cinched tighter than a rodeo horse.

'Well, if it ain't the double-crossing cowboy.' Wafting of strong perfume and swinging a parasol, Pearl stood at the end of the bed, a smirk on her painted lips. 'Hear tell you're a one-armed cripple these days. Seems like you got your just desserts.'

'You think so?' Zeke, awoken from sleep, was taken aback by her sudden appearance. 'You double-crossed me first.'

'Me? How come?'

'With Beauregard and the judge.'

'That was business. How do you think I pay for these latest Paris fashions?'

Pearl bounced down on the bed, her summer dress rustling suggestively, its front cut low to reveal her milky white bosom. She crooked-up a leg to show off her high-buttoned bootees and hitched-up her white kid gloves to the elbows. 'So, who's sorry now?' she cooed, sticking out her little pink tongue at him.

Zeke could not help but feel a lick of his old fiery feeling for her, but it turned to anger as he reached for his Smith & Wesson. 'If all you've come here for is to crow, you better git out quick 'cause I can still use a gun with my right hand, and I've a mind to put a bullet through that cheatin' heart of yourn.'

'Now, now, darlin', don't get het up just 'cause you can't git your oats. Yes, I can tell you want to. But I ain't int'rested in penniless has-been cripples.'

She quickly removed herself from the bed when

Zeke cocked the revolver and aimed it at her. 'OK, I'm going. Why should I want to stay? I s'pose you thought you'd get me put in jail, too? Well, your li'l trick didn't work. Ha! Ha!'

'You can tell that murderin' Cherokee I'm ready for him, too,' Zeke shouted, as she exited. 'Any time.'

When she had gone he swung to his feet and glowered at his image in the fly-specked mirror. 'Wow! The cheek of the dame. I need me a whiskey.'

'They've stabbed me in the back,' Judge Parker bemoaned to his court when the Supreme Court began opening the door to appeals. Of forty persons doomed by him to hang who took their case to Washington, thirty were judged victims of unfair trials; sixteen won acquittals and the other fourteen got off with prison terms.

'There should be no reversals at all unless innocence is manifest. Murderers are being released for absurd legal technicalities,' he said. 'I, myself, would brush aside all technicalities that do not affect the guilt or innocence of the accused.'

But the Hanging Judge's powers were being curbed. One of those to benefit was Belle Starr who was freed after only six months of incarceration. While her husband was still doing time in federal prison at Detroit, Belle took up with a Texan thug, John Middleton, on the lam after a cold-blooded murder in his home state.

After Sam Starr was released, Middleton's body was found on the bank of the Poteau River and most men were of the opinion that the Cherokee had caught up with him and left him there. Like his father he held strong grudges. In spite of his pretence of affability most deemed it unwise to cross him.

In the fall, Marshal Thomas made another visit to Widow Roff's homestead in the lonesome Ouachita forest, riding through Big Cedar, crossing the Kiamichi mountains and following Eagle Fork Creek. He had another rookie side-kick now, Deputy Marshal Ike Isabel and, as they rode they heard the roaring of rutting bucks up in the pines, clashing antlers for dominance of their harems.

'Animals and humans, they all got this demonic urge to procreate,' the marshal drawled. 'Bucks do it once a year. It's a pity humans couldn't, too.'

Deputy Isabel piped up, 'You seem to have a

poor opinion of humanity, Heck.'

'The ones I meet is there any wonder?' the marshal mused. 'Soon as one killer's gone, Jesse James, Sam Bass, and so on, another springs up to fill his shoes.'

The forest was a patchwork of fall colours, the days darkening and chill. Soon the hills would be mantled in snow. The willowy Ice was still at the ranch although Alva Roff had withdrawn his men. She made them welcome in her kitchen.

'We're on the lookout for Ned Christie,' Heck explained. 'We've had another big setback. Frank Dalton's been killed by three rum peddlers he went after. I guess his brothers will run 'em down and exact their own vengeance. But this just goes to show the trouble booze-hawking causes. Christie started off like that but now he's graduated to robbing and killing.'

'I am glad to say I have seen no sign of him,' Ice replied. 'He's a Cherokee, isn't he?'

'Yes. It's bad enough having all these white criminals hiding out in the Nations, but now a helluva lot of full-blood, half-blood and blacks are turning bad.'

Ice shrugged as she poured them coffee in her kitchen. 'What do you expect? You whites

143

slaughtered all our buffalo, took our livelihood, stole our land. Not long ago our young men would take pride in being warriors, horsemen, hunters. Now, what is there for them?'

'I guess that's true,' Heck sighed, and offered her a wild turkey he had shot. 'Maybe if I pluck and clean it we could eat it tonight?'

It was getting late and they were hungry as hunters ought to be by time the turkey was cooked. Showing the skills she had learned at convent school, Ice served it up with cranberry sauce and sweet potatoes.

When he was full and warm by the stove Heck tamped his pipe. 'Are you planning on staying here?' he asked the girl.

'I'm not sure,' Ice replied. 'Alva has deemed it unprofitable to run his cattle on this ranch so I'm seriously thinking of going back to my tribe.'

'It must be hard for a woman to cope out here in the wilderness on her own. To tell the truth I wanted to explain to you about Zeke.'

'How is he?' Ice's dark eyes lit up. 'I heard he had been wounded.'

'He ain't too good,' Deputy Isabel put in. 'He's taken it hard, the loss of his arm. He's hanging around the saloons of Fort Smith, drinkin'' whiskey, feelin' sorry for himself.'

'He told me he was going to marry Pearl Starr.'

'No, I don't think Pearl's interested in him now,' Heck said. 'He ain't got enough cash. I was wondering about you, Ice? When we was last here he seemed purty well struck by you.'

'I don't blame him,' Ike yelped, admiring the comely Indian girl somewhat lecherously.

'Me?'

'Yeah.' Heck frowned at his deputy. 'That boy needs someone to believe in him. I rode for two months with him and I can vouch he's as brave as a bobcat and straight as six o'clock.'

Ice gave a slight smile. 'Perhaps you can tell Zeke I will wait here for him until the snows come. Then I must go.'

SIXTEEN

A light veil of snow was falling, the first of winter, and the air ice sharp as Zeke gigged his stallion on towards the blaze of lights that was Vinita since the coming of the railroad.

'This used to be the hellhole of the Nations,' an Indian deputy marshal, Dan Blackfeather, told him. 'Now it is even hotter. The trains bring girls from the Kansan cattle towns, gamblers, gunmen, pickpockets, mug-hunters, thieves and murderers, all sharp-eyed to make big bucks.'

Zeke, who had fallen in with the deputy on the trail, was leading two Appaloosa mares and two foals he had purchased for $300 from a travelling circus man in Wichita.

He didn't need to hitch the mares. They gladly

trotted after his stallion which had already covered them. 'Old Spot can't believe his luck,' Zeke said, with a grin, as the stallion went prancing and whinnying along proudly.

Zeke had pulled himself out of his apathy at Fort Smith and decided he would make something of himself, be a horse dealer in Appaloosas like his daddy before him.

They rode into Vinita's main street which was a muddy turmoil of wagons and horses, piles of rubbish and lumber, with ramshackle stores along the sidewalks on either side. A livery sign said, 'Two dollars a night, hay and grain', so they booked their horses in and went looking for nourishment for themselves.

At one end of the street was a sturdy 'Katy' locomotive, steaming and hissing, sending a shower of sparks out of its tall stack into the night. The K & T, proposed Kansas to Texas line, had reached Vinita and stopped amid its jumble of construction supplies while more land treaties were negotiated with the tribes.

'There's so much booze peddled in now we have to turn a blind eye to it,' Dan explained, as they shouldered their way through the crowd and glanced in numerous establishments from which music and women's laughter drifted. 'Otherwise we would have no time to pursue criminals.'

'Yeah?' In the light of a tar flare Zeke stood outside a white-painted wooden place with the single word, 'Harry's' over the entrance. 'Who you pursuin' in partic'lar, Dan?'

'Sam Starr. He robbed the Creek treasury and we believe he's headed this way.'

'Sam Starr?' It was as if his useless arm suddenly twitched at the name. 'Now that interests me.'

They went inside and found a table to one side with a view of the bar. Harry, himself, was a prosperous, well-fed gent, in an apron and shirt-sleeves, his hair parted in the centre and looping away on either side to match his giant moustachios. 'What's it to be, boys?' he drawled, as he introduced himself. 'Venison stew suit you? I shot it myself.'

Zeke, with his good arm, propped his Winchester against the wall. 'Suits me.'

'How about drinks.' Harry gave a wink. 'Lookin' for anything a little stronger?'

'Not me.' Dan pulled his blanket coat to one side to reveal his badge. 'I'm on duty.'

Harry suddenly didn't look so amiable. 'Don't get me wrong. I—'

148

'Yeah, sure,' Dan replied. 'Don't worry about it.' It was pretty obvious that a gang of raucous railroadmen up at the bar were tippling mugs of gin, rum or whiskey. 'I ain't here for that.'

'In that case I'll have a beer.' Zeke smiled. 'I ain't in the service. Don't wanna git arrested, but I'll risk it.'

When his belly was full, Zeke leaned back and studied the prairie angels up at the bar, Indian, coffee-coloured and white. One, dressed much like Pearl, if not so expensively, gave him a cheeky grin. Zeke ran his fingers through his fair thatch and shook his head, regretfully. 'Not tonight, Josephine.'

Dan noticed. 'You don't like the ladies?'

'It ain't that I ain't tempted. The gal's kinda sweet. An old-fashioned alley cat, just like Pearl. It's just that I don't fancy a cold 'tween the legs, as you Injuns quaintly put it. I'm keeping myself for someone classier.'

'Who would that be?' But Dan suddenly put out his hand to restrain Zeke's good arm. 'Do you see who I see?'

'Sure do.' The former deputy's heart had started to pound hard at the sight of the man who had crippled him. 'Talk of the devil!'

149

Old Tom Starr had caused so much bloodshed the Cherokee tribal council had signed a treaty with him, granting him tribute money as well as amnesty for past crimes, in return for lawful behaviour.

Since then his son, Sam, had turned his attentions instead to the Creeks. And here was the tall, slim Cherokee himself. His long hair held by a headband, in his black suit and white shirt, he stepped into Harry's bar. The problem for Dan was he had two sidekicks in tow, a big, bicep-bulging black fellow, garbed in just a waistcoat and pants beneath a caped topcoat, and a surly 'breed in a battered Lincoln hat, dusty suit and boots.

All were carrying bulging saddle-bags which no doubt contained stolen Creek gold and silver. They threw them into a corner, intent on a good time with whiskey and girls. Zeke and Dan Blackfeather in their shadowy corner beyond a tar torch flickering in its holder on the wall went unnoticed.

'You gonna arrest 'em?' Zeke hissed. 'I'll side you.'

'It ain't nuthin' to do with you,' Dan muttered. 'I can take 'em.'

There was a worried, but fatalistic look to the

Indian's features as he unbuttoned his holster, pulled a revolver half out and got to his feet. He moved to position himself at the far end of the bar on the other side of the fancy ladies and the railroadmen.

'Sam Starr,' Dan shouted. 'Hold it right there. You're under arrest.'

The Cherokee already had a mug of whiskey in one hand and the other arm around the girl who had smiled at Zeke. He tightened his grip on her and pulled her to cover him. 'What the hell you talking about?' He put the mug aside, pulling his revolver from his belt.

'You other two,' Dan said. 'I'm taking you in, too. Raise your hands.'

'How you gonna do that?' The black guy gave a deep chuckle as the railroadmen and other girls quickly moved out of the line of fire.

'Yeah.' The 'breed stealthily drew a big scalping knife. 'You asking for trouble, mister?'

'He's gonna do it 'cause I'm gonna help him.' Zeke got to his feet, his good hand hovering over the butt of his Smith & Wesson. 'Remember me, Sam?'

'You!' Starr gave a surprised sneer. 'You're just a useless cripple. We made sure of that.'

'Who? You or Belle?'

The Cherokee flashed his white teeth. 'That would be telling. You ain't a deputy any more. You got no authority—'

'Maybe I ain't got no licence to kill, but that don't bother me,' Zeke replied hoarsely. 'A cowardly crawling rat like you needs putting down. So what's it to be? A tight necktie at Fort Smith? Or shall we finish it?'

Sam Starr began making a weird turkey gobble sound, the Cherokee death chant, so they knew his answer. The top-hatted 'breed hurled his knife. Zeke ducked as Sam fired, too. Lead and steel thudded into the wall behind him. Zeke hurled the tar flare to scatter them.

Suddenly the bar was a cauldron of explosions, gunflashes and smoke as Deputy Blackfeather, Sam Starr, Zeke and the 'breed began blasting away. Zeke tried to get a shot at Sam but feared he might hit the girl. He aimed his Smith & Wesson at the 'breed instead, who grimaced as he caught lead in the thigh.

Blackfeather, however, swapped lead with Sam. The girl screamed and went limp in Sam's arm. He dropped her and put a hole through Blackfeather's heart to send him crashing to the floor.

The black's eyes bulged as he hauled out a sawn-off shotgun from his coat and let loose a spray of lead to pepper the wall. Zeke dived for cover under a table. The last two bullets from his self-cocker knocked the shotgun flying and catapulted the shooter into eternity.

Flames from the flare started to lick up behind the bar. Maybe this or whiskey, or panic affected Starr's aim. His shots at Zeke whistled wide. Zeke had a clear target but he was out of lead. He rolled over and made a grab for his Winchester, ready-primed with a bullet in the spout. He pulled it tight into his good shoulder and took out the Cherokee. Sam's turkey gobble became a gasp of shock as blood spouted from his chest and he hit the deck.

'Any more for any more?' Zeke, unable to lever another slug into the breech with only one hand, quickly abandoned his carbine and got hold of Dan's, instead. He peered through the smoke from the tar flare and the rolling clouds of black cordite at the five bodies on the bar floor. Suddenly the wounded half-breed raised himself, firing a shot from a six-gun which whistled past Zeke's ear. He held the carbine steady and smashed a slug into the 'breed's forehead. 'Go to hell.'

The chubby whore was still alive, but fading fast. 'Why?' was all she could say.

'I dunno,' Zeke replied, comforting her as blood trickled from her pale lips. He made the sign of the cross over her, as her eyes closed. 'Guess you were just in the wrong place at the wrong time. You're goin' to a better place, sweetheart. At least, that's what I'm told.'

'Just look!' – Harry was hurling buckets of water at the flames – protesting. 'What a mess you've made off my bar! You trying to ruin me?'

'Yeah. Robbed you of some lucrative custom, no doubt.' Zeke gave a grin of sheer relief, feeling as nervy as a cat and twice as jumpy. Folks were coming back to life, so to speak, marvelling at the five corpses on the floor lying in their widening pools of blood.

'Waal,' Zeke drawled, poking Sam Starr with his boot. 'You ain't got the use of *any* limbs now, have you, buddy? Guess I won.'

He went to the bar and finished off the Cherokee's whiskey. 'I'll take Dan Blackfeather, their saddle-bags and hosses. You can do what you like with the others. So long. Nice meeting you folks.'

*

Thick snow had laid a white mantle upon the mountainsides as he followed the trail along Eagle Creek. It was globbing the pine branches, tumbling on him as he and his Appaloosas brushed past. He had dropped off Dan Blackfeather, the outlaws' horses, guns, and saddle-bags full of stolen silver and gold, precious artefacts and ornaments, at the big two-storey, sandstone Council House of the Creek Nation at Okmulgee, much to the chief's surprise, and gone on his way.

Ice was busy loading a wagon with household goods as he cantered into the ranch-house yard. There was surprise and hesitation in her dark lustrous eyes as she spoke. 'I am going back to my people.'

'Wouldn't you rather stay? I got the start here of a nice herd of Appaloosas.' He had been more or less born in the saddle and riding one-handed didn't bother him. He swung lightly down and confronted her. 'If you don't mind marryin' a one-armed man.'

'All I want is you.' Ice nestled into him, rubbing her cold nose against his. 'I've waited a long time. But a big grizzly has been nosing about. He frightens me.'

155

'I've just killed Sam Starr and his two *compadres*,' he muttered. 'So a big ol' grizzly ain't gonna bother me. He better watch out. I ain't averse to a nice bear steak. And his coat'll make a warm cover for our bed.'

Ice pressed her slim body into him and touched his paralysed hand, which seemed to give a twitch. 'Perhaps you will get life back in it one day.'

'I got plenty of life in my other extremity.' He grabbed her tight. 'That'll be plenty good enough for us to while away the winter nights. Shall we git in outa the cold?'

Snow speckled her black hair like jewels as Ice nodded and tears filled her eyes. 'That's all I want, Zeke. To make love to you. To bear your children. I believe it is destined.'

AUTHOR'S NOTE

Some cynics say the Wild West was just a myth. But the fact is sixty-five US marshals and deputies were killed during the twenty-one years of Judge Parker's reign. Fort Smith's jurisdiction was larger than that of any other court in history. Its law officers killed or captured more murderous outlaws than any comparable group. Not many of their opponents survived. Belle Starr was shot from her saddle by a hidden assassin as she rode along the bank of the Canadian River. Suspicion fell on her new Indian lover, Jim July. He resisted arrest and died in a gun duel with Heck Thomas. Ned Christie was finally cornered by Heck and his boys and riddled with bullets. The marshal then went after another norious outlaw, Bill Doolin, shot-

gunned him and decimated his gang. Hangman
Maledon was not immune to tragedy. His
daughter, Annie, 18, was murdered by a jealous
suitor. Both the judge and Maledon were incensed
that her killer escaped the noose on appeal.
Maledon left Fort Smith never to return. The
'carnival of hangings' came to an end when Judge
Parker was relieved of his command. By the turn of
the century the Indian Nations had been opened
to settlement and re-named Oklahoma where
Pearl Starr became madame of a bawdy house.
Two badmen who survived, Cole Younger and Grat
Dalton became reformed men after release from
jail. And after more than fifty years of fearlessly
facing bullets, Heck Thomas, marshal of Lawton,
Oklahoma, died of natural causes, aged sixty-two.
This story was a fictional re-imagining of those days
based on true events.